DISNEY DESCENDANTS 2

MAL'S

~~Maleficent's~~

SPELL BOOK

ADAPTED BY TINA McLEEF

BASED ON THE FILM BY

JOSANN McGIBBON & SARA PARRIOTT

WAVES OF TROUBLE

DISNEP PRESS

LOS ANGELES • NEW YORK

THREE days UNTil COTillioN. COTillioN, a.k.a. AURaDON PREP'S BiggEST PARTY of THE YEAR, a.k.a. GET DRESSED UP aND PRETEND TO BE SOMEONE YOU'RE NOT.

An Inheritance

I'M goiNg aS BEN'S date, of COURSE, aND THAT'S STill THE bEST PART. BEN'S lEARNiNg THE ROPES aS KiNg, aND I lOVE SPENDiNG TiME WiTH HiM, BUT iT'S alSO bEEN a liTTlE ... UM ... iNTENSE.

IS THERE a MORE iNTENSE woRD FOR "iNTENSE"?

The child of a villain
Has their legacy to uphold,
A reputation for evil deeds,
The revulsion of the masses.

As a reminder of this,
The villain child may inherit
A token of the parent's lack of affection
And their endless yearning for power.

BECaUSE THAT'S WHaT iT'S bEEN likE. I'VE bEEN iN AURaDON FOR a liTTlE WHilE NOW, aND iT waS REally HaRD TO FiT iN aT FiRST, ESPECially WiTH all THiS Talk of "MANNERS" aND "gOODNESS." THaT iSN'T HOW I waS RaiSED. KiND of THE OPPOSiTE, actually. I FOUND THiS book, THoUgH, CallED A LADY'S MANNERS, aND iT'S REally HElPED. ⟶

The items bequeathed may include:

I've also been using my spell book still (I know, I know, Evie!), and some of the spells have helped, too. People are starting to see me as the perfect princess, and cotillion is when I officially become lady of the court. Everyone's saying I've come a really long way from who I used to be.... I guess that's supposed to be a good thing. Should I really be celebrating, though?
—Mal

Emerald Brooch

Scepter

Treasure Chest

Poison Apple

Iron Hook

Magical Golden Flower

Hooded Cloak

JAY HERE. DON'T WORRY, MAL, IT HASN'T BEEN EASY FOR ME, EITHER. THERE ARE LIKE **TEN GIRLS** WHO WANT ME TO TAKE THEM TO COTILLION....

IT'S NOT FAIR! YOU ARE ONE PERSON. WHY DO YOU HAVE A HUNDRED INVITES TO COTILLION?
—CARLOS

WATCH AND LEARN, MAN.

Mal. Do NOT sweat this. You've been doing a crazy-good job! You looked like a pro on that news clip this morning.
—Evie

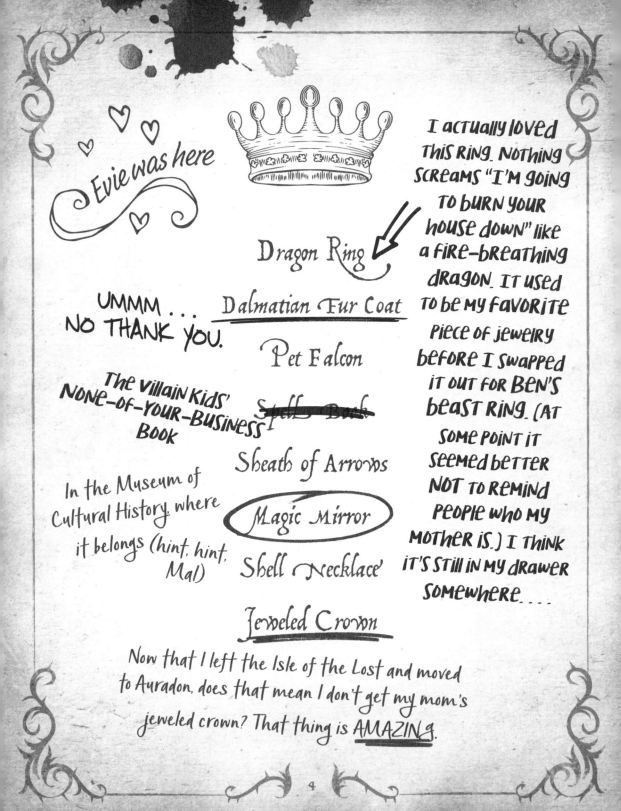

Evie was here

Dragon Ring

I actually loved this ring. Nothing screams "I'M GOING TO BURN YOUR HOUSE DOWN" like a FIRE-BREATHING DRAGON. IT USED TO BE MY FAVORITE piece of jewelry before I swapped it out for BEN'S beast ring. (AT SOME POINT IT SEEMED BETTER NOT TO REMIND PEOPLE WHO MY MOTHER IS.) I THINK IT'S STILL IN MY DRAWER SOMEWHERE . . . .

UMMM . . . NO THANK YOU.

Dalmatian Fur Coat

Pet Falcon

The Villain Kids' NONE-OF-YOUR-BUSINESS ~~Spell Book~~ Book

Sheath of Arrows

In the Museum of Cultural History where it belongs (hint, hint, Mal)

Magic Mirror

Shell Necklace

Jeweled Crown

Now that I left the Isle of the Lost and moved to Auradon, does that mean I don't get my mom's jeweled crown? That thing is AMAZING.

A BOX THAT YOU KEEP A PRINCESS'S HEART IN? YOUR MOM IS MORE THAN A LITTLE CREEPY.

Your dad isn't perfect, either....

TOUCHÉ.

Prepping for Cotillion has been stressful, but this has been the best month yet for my Evie's 4 Hearts business. We're drowning in rubies and emeralds from all the custom gown orders I've gotten. Just today a reporter was talking about my designs, saying (this is a real quote) I was "Auradon's hottest new designer." How's that for amazing advertising? Girls have been lining up outside my door. This is the land of opportunity!!! I feel like I'm really making the most of it....

Bronze Cauldron

Heart Box

Sword

Serpent Staff

Cane

THINK THIS COULD DOUBLE AS A SWORD? I ALWAYS THOUGHT IT WAS COOL.

IAGO IS A LUNATIC. **I DO NOT** WANT THAT BIRD!

Pet Parrot

Wig

Scrying Bowl

COME ON.
EVEN IF
IT'S CRÈME
BRÛLÉE?!

HEY, MAL,
REMEMBER THAT
TIME YOU HAD
DINNER WITH
ALADDIN AND
JASMINE AND YOU
SPIT THAT CHUNK
OF MEAT INTO YOUR
HAND? AND THE
CAMERAS CAUGHT IT
AND THEY PLAYED
IT ON TV ABOUT A
DOZEN TIMES?

I'VE BEEN
TRYING TO
FORGET
THAT EVER
HAPPENED. . . .
THANKS, JAY.

∽ A Lady's Manners ∽

Dinner Etiquette for Ladies

A lady is <u>always on time for dinner.</u>   I NEVER EVEN HAD A
WATCH ON THE ISLE,
A lady does not taste another person's food.   AND THAT'S HOW
I LIKED IT.

A lady always sits up straight.

A lady would never dare put her elbows on the table.

A lady never bites into a whole piece of bread. Instead, she tears off small pieces.

If a lady has the great misfortune of having a piece of food stuck in her teeth, she goes to the powder room to remove it. She never tells a soul.

If a bite of food is not to a lady's liking, she discreetly transfers it from her mouth into her napkin. She never makes a scene.

A lady never laughs too loudly, talks too loudly, or draws unwanted attention to her table.

TRY TO KEEP LAUGHING TO A MINIMUM.

∽ 8 ∽

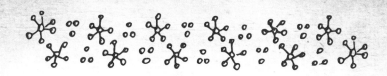

The Evil Eye

A piercing stare
Meant to do harm:
Protect yourself
With this good luck charm.

I need to get one of these, stat. Have you seen how some of those paparazzi look at me?

They're not the friendliest bunch....

Eating Tricky Foods With Grace

Banana: There is only one way to eat an unpeeled banana. Slice off both ends with a sharp knife. Make a long cut down the center of the peel, then fold it open. <u>Slice and eat the fruit with a knife and fork.</u>

Berries: Eat berries with a spoon if they do not have stems. If they do have stems, you may pick them up by the stem. Never, under any circumstances, spear with a fork.

Cake: It is acceptable to eat cake with your fingers only if it is cut into bite-sized pieces. If it is iced or sticky or comes with ice cream, you must use a fork and spoon. The spoon should go in your right hand and will scoop up the dessert. The fork will go in your left hand and should gently push the piece onto the spoon. (The key word is "gently"—never use too much force.)

Spaghetti: It is unforgivable to cut spaghetti with your knife. Instead, eat only a few strands at a time, twirling them tightly around your fork.

~❧ 16 ❧~

I ONLY **JUST** GOT USED TO USING UTENSILS AT THE DINNER TABLE, AND NOW THIS? THERE'S STILL SO MUCH TO LEARN....

WAIT . . . YOU HAVE TO CUT A BANANA WITH A KNIFE AND FORK?! SINCE WHEN? I ONLY EVEN LEARNED ABOUT THE <u>INSIDE</u> OF THE BANANA WHEN I GOT TO AURADON!

Yeah, back on the Isle I always wondered what used to be inside the old ROTTEN PEELS they gave us for snacks when we were little.

Anyway, I wouldn't have known any of this stuff if it weren't for my "Lady's Manner's" book. And the rule about spaghetti?! The first time I ate with Belle and King Beast I cut it with a knife. I'm not sure if they saw, but either way, it's humiliating.

I know we didn't grow up with manners, or silverware, or formal dining and three-course meals . . . but this does seem a little extreme. I checked with Doug and he said we can eat our bananas however we want.

WE DIDN'T GROW UP WITH VEGETABLES . . . OR FRUIT!

A Lady's Manners

Olives: If an olive is pitted, eat it whole. If the olive is large and has a pit, eat it in small bites. As for the pit, discreetly place it on the edge of your plate. You should never, under any circumstances, spit it into your hand.

Peas: It is impolite to scoop up your peas. They must be speared with your fork and eaten in small bites.

Soup: You must always scoop your soupspoon away from you. Then sip from the nearside of the spoon. <u>Do not slurp your soup</u> or drink it from the bowl. Ever.

I WANT TO BE SUPPORTIVE, MAL, BUT SOME OF THIS STUFF JUST SEEMS CRAZY. NEVER, UNDER ANY CIRCUMSTANCES, SPEAR A BERRY WITH A FORK? WHAT'S SO BAD ABOUT THAT? AND WHY IS IT OKAY TO SPEAR PEAS BUT NOT BERRIES? AND DO I HAVE TO EAT MY PEAS AT ALL? THEY'RE ALMOST AS BAD AS THE BARNACLES WE ATE ON THE ISLE. THIS MAKES

NO SENSE!

AND HAS ANYONE ELSE TRIED OLIVES YET? ARE THOSE THE WEIRD LITTLE THINGS WITH PITS?

I tried them! They're kind of salty and gross. Tasted like home.

Jay, I agree, but this is just basic stuff that everyone in Auradon knows except for us. It's so much pressure, having to eat dinner with ten cameras watching when there are all these intricate rules.

IT would be kind of cool to have a CRYSTAL ball RIGHT NOW. I haven't even seen one since I left the Isle....

Crystal Balls

Crystal balls have been used
For divination since the beginning of time.
Gaze into the sparkling depths of the orb
And see the future as it unfolds.
Spheres of moss agate
Are best for seeing the coming days,
While those of rose quartz
Are best for foretelling the years ahead.

UM ... IS THAT ME?
IS THIS REAL LIFE?!

THE FUTURE LADY OF THE COURT

King Ben steps out with his girlfriend, Lady Mal. In just a few days she will be named lady of the court at Auradon's royal cotillion.

BEST "MAL MOMENTS" CAUGHT ON CAMERA

1. THAT TIME SHE STEPPED ON FAIRY GODMOTHER'S FOOT.
2. THAT TIME SHE SHOT A PEA INTO MULAN'S EYE. ← I was trying to spear it!
3. THAT TIME SHE SPILLED TEA IN HER LAP.
4. THAT TIME SHE TRIED TO AWKWARDLY DANCE WITH KING BEAST. ← That wasn't my fault!
5. THAT TIME SHE SMILED WITH SPINACH IN HER TEETH FOR THE DURATION OF BELLE'S LUNCHEON.

They said we were SUPPOSED to dance. They never said what *kind* of dance.

Reading Spell

Take these words upon the page
And have me know them like a sage.

Read it fast at lightning speed,
Remember everything I need.

Don't forget what I've been told,
'Cause knowledge is wisdom's gold.

We won't take this personally!

I THINK JANE MAY BE THE (PRETTIEST GIRL) IN SCHOOL. AND SHE'S SO KIND, TOO. JUST YESTERDAY I WAS TRYING TO ASK HER TO COTILLION . . . BUT THEN I ASKED HER IF SHE LIKED THE DESSERT IN THE DINING HALL, INSTEAD. I DON'T KNOW WHAT TO DO. WHENEVER I'M AROUND HER, I GET SO TONGUE-TIED. A LITTLE HELP, PLEASE? ANYONE?

Just be yourself.

Seriously, Carlos—you're awesome.

DITTO.

I GOT YOU, BUD.

WAYS TO IMPRESS AURADON PREP GIRLS

1. STRUT. KEEP YOUR SHOULDERS BACK AND YOUR CHIN UP, AND ALWAYS WALK WITH CONFIDENCE.

2. PRETEND YOU DON'T NOTICE THEM. IF A GIRL THINKS YOU'RE TOO EAGER, SHE'S NOT GOING TO BE INTERESTED.

This is not true, Carlos! One of my favorite things about Doug is that he really sees me and gets me. He cares about me and about us. Girls love that.

3. PLAY A SPORT. GIRLS LOVE ATHLETIC GUYS.

4. LOOK GOOD. GIRLS LOVE GUYS WITH STYLE.

Also false! I like Doug because he's interesting and smart. He doesn't have to play a sport to be cool.

5. KEEP YOUR OPTIONS OPEN. DON'T CHOOSE A COTILLION DATE UNLESS YOU ABSOLUTELY HAVE TO.

I'M WITH EVIE. AURADON MUST BE TURNING ME INTO A SERIOUS SOFTY, BECAUSE MY FIRST THOUGHT WAS:

JUST FOLLOW YOUR HEART, CARLOS.

DON'T TRY TO PLAY GAMES.
GIRLS DON'T LIKE IT.

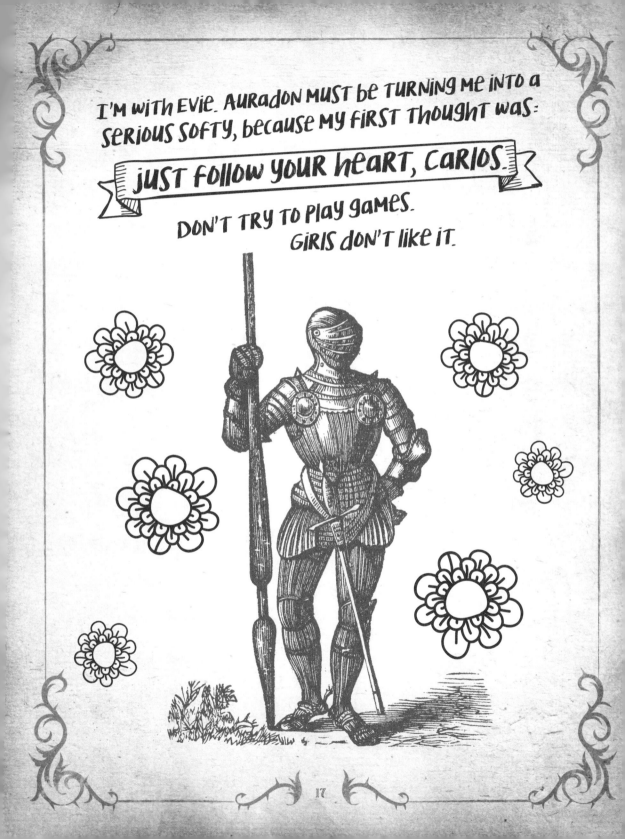

Essential Oils

Oils are best made
On the night of a crescent moon,
The substance boiled in water
From an enchanted lake,
Simmered for hours until slick little beads
Float to the top to be strained,
Bottled, and stored for future use.

GUYS! The cotillion is taking over my life! When I'm not being hunted by the paparazzi, Jane is trailing behind me, asking me a hundred questions about the ice sculptures, and the band, and the chair swag.

And now I just found out that going to cotillion with Ben is like being "engaged to be engaged." I haven't even graduated high school yet, and I'm supposed to know who I want to marry? How has my whole life been planned out for me without me even realizing?

ALMOST all MY life I've been a villain kid. I've only barely gotten the hang of fitting in here in Auradon, of etiquette and dressing the part of the PRIM, PROPER lady. . . . CAN'T I PLEASE have ONE MINUTE TO BREATHE?

Okay . . . just one minute. Because we really need to have another fitting for your Cotillion dress. I want to make sure I got your measurements right. and I still need to figure out the accessories.

Helichrysum: Healing, regenerative

Ho Wood: Headache relief

Does anyone have some HO WOOD OIL I can borrow?

Jasmine: Calming properties

Juniper berry: antiseptic properties

Palmarosa: treatment of fevers

Black pepper: invigorating, decongestant

Tea tree: supports immune health

Clove: bug repellant

Vetiver: tranquility

If you told the old me I'd be DESPERATE FOR a little TRANQUILITY, I never would have believed you. . . .

You're doing great, Mal, just hang in there. Cotillion is only a few days away!

The Lady's Closet: Dressing Like a Lady

Every lady should own a dress for daytime wear, a slim pair of trousers, and an evening gown. When in doubt, think simple and timeless.

BLAH, BLAH, BLAH.

Stick with classic styles. Bows and tulle are flattering on everyone. Pastels go well with so many different skin tones.

When it comes to accessories, less is more. Do not layer necklaces or belts. Never wear more than one ring on each hand. **HA!**

Wear dresses and skirts whenever possible. Nothing announces a lady like a beautiful dress.

A good pair of heels is a must for any lady. A pair of ballet flats may suffice when heels are not possible.

DO YOU THINK MY STUDDED BOOTS WITH CHUNKY HEELS COUNT?

≈ 82 ≈

Dresses are skirts are great but they're forgetting about **LEGGINGS.** Love those!

This is <u>nonsense</u>! No layering necklaces? Only <u>one</u> ring?!

DON'T SHOOT THE MESSENGER . . . .

Speaking of dressing like a lady, my Evie's 4 Hearts business is booming. Just today, Doug and I ran the numbers for all the Cotillion dresses I've been commissioned to create, and if things keep going this way, I'll be able to buy my own castle soon. Right now I'm designing Cotillion gowns for Lonnie, Jane, Mal, and myself, and then outfits for all the guys, plus dozens of other Auradon Prep students. I can barely keep all the orders straight.

For once I feel like my life is really going somewhere. Days on the Isle went by so slowly, each one the same as the one before, but here it's different ... it's exciting. For once I am really crazy excited.

Dressing Like a Villain Kid

-Always layer accessories: necklaces, scarves, bracelets, and rings. There's no such thing as too many.

-Experiment with color and cut—the more unique, the better.

-Don't be afraid to try new styles and fabrics. Break away from the pack of pretty princesses all wearing the same poufy gown.

-Wear what makes you feel like YOU. Pants are great. Boots are great. Jackets, capes, and high collars are excellent options. Don't feel like you need to look like someone else.

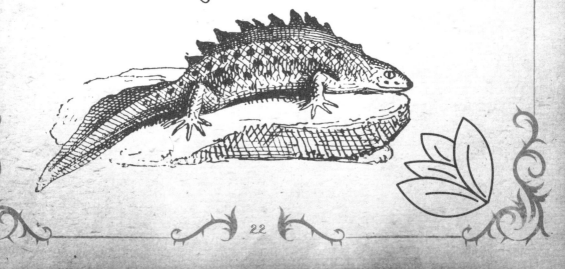

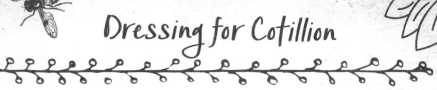

Dressing for Cotillion

-DO choose unusual accessories. Statement rings, bows, brooches chains, and belts can all pair nicely with an evening gown.

-DON'T be afraid to be bold. Nothing makes a statement like a bright color.

-DO coordinate with your date. Choose patterns, colors, and fabrics that complement each other.

-DON'T wait until the last minute to commission your dress. Designers may be booked up to two months in advance.

-DO consider having a custom purse designed. A stunning purse or clutch can complete your look.

-DON'T forget to decide on a hairstyle. Different gowns call for different looks, and a good stylist can point you in the right direction.

Scarabs

Scarabs, iridescent and beautiful,
Are a symbol of destiny and fate.
They will come to you
When the path ahead is split
And there is a choice to make.

MAL, HOW'S
YOUR MOM
DOING? DOES
SHE LIKE BEING
A LIZARD?

A FEW TIMES
I'VE CAUGHT
HER PACING HER
CAGE, PLOTTING,
BUT OTHER THAN
THAT, SHE'S
PRETTY MELLOW.

Journey on, traveler,
But know your next steps
Must be filled with intention,
For the path you choose
Will forever change your destiny.

BEING CAPTAIN OF THE R.O.A.R. TEAM IS NO JOKE.
WE'VE BEEN PRACTICING EVERY DAY AFTER SCHOOL, AND
I'M STILL LEARNING NEW TECHNIQUES. YESTERDAY A
KID FROM SHERWOOD FOREST DID A WICKED LUNGE
AT ME. I DUCKED AND THREW MY SHIELD UP JUST IN
TIME TO BLOCK HIM.

IT'S A REAL CHANGE
FROM LIFE ON THE
ISLE.... THERE
WEREN'T
REALLY ANY
TEAMS.
THERE WASN'T
ANYONE
WATCHING YOUR
BACK. IT WAS EVERY
VILLAIN FOR HIMSELF.
I'M WITH EVIE—I HAVE TO
ADMIT, AURADON HAS SOME DEFINITE PLUSSES.
MAYBE IT'S NOT PERFECT, BUT IT'S CLOSE.

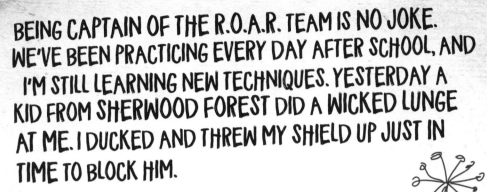

I'M glad you guys are
happy here....

DOES THAT MEAN
YOU'RE NOT?

MAL?

A Spell for a Feast

SO IN all THE
COTILLION
CHAOS, I TOTally
FORGOT THAT
BEN AND I MADE
a PLAN TO GO TO
THE ENCHANTED
Lake. I GUESS
I PROMISED
TO MAKE HIM a
FEAST? AND WE
WERE DEFINITELY
GOING TO GO ON
THURSDAY, WHICH
IS APPARENTLY
TODAY!?!

A single grape,
An uncooked steak,
A pot of porridge cold and wet:
Turn the ordinary
Into the extraordinary
And make your most
impressive meal yet.

In a large bowl
of white marble
Set down a morsel of food.
Cover with a cloth woven from
the hair of stallions
And incant these words:

And don't forget
you have another
fitting for your
Cotillion dress at
5 p.m. sharp!
Don't be late!
There are already
a dozen girls
waiting outside.
(But you know the
designer, and if she
absolutely has to,
she can sneak you
in first....)

Ugh. I searched through the stash of snacks I keep under my bed, and all I have is a jar of peanut butter, three packets of jelly, and two slices of day-old bread. Evie donated a cookie to my cause, but it looks pretty pathetic, even when I put it all together on a fancy plate. It's not a feast—not even close. I ran as fast as I could to the dining hall, but I got there just in time to see them lock the doors. It won't open again until dinnertime.

I know I shouldn't be using my spell book in Auradon. I do know that. But I just flipped

Simple to savory,
Desiccated to divine,
Transform this dish into a delectable feast
And let us dine together in glory.

through the pages and I happened upon this spell . . . and I really could use a little help right now. Would it be so terrible if I turned these measly morsels into something more impressive? Maybe a rack of lamb or crème brûlée?

What Ben doesn't know won't hurt him, Right?

The Lady's Guide
to Setting the Table

Water glass ✓

Goblet ✓

Salad plate

Napkin ✓

Salad fork ✓

Dinner fork ✓

Dinner plate ✓

Dinner knife ✓

Soupspoon ✓

Dessert spoon

BORROW PICNIC baSKeT FROM JaNe.

88

NOTE TO SELF:
DO NOT FORGET THE DESSERT SPOONS.

IT'S AN EVEN-NUMBERED DAY, MAL. WHAT DID THAT HANDSOME KING GIVE YOU NOW? A GOOSE THAT LAYS GOLDEN EGGS? MAGIC BEANS?

AM I the ONLY PERSON who didn't Realize Ben gets me PRESENTS every other day, on just the even ones? HOW did I NOT NOTICE THAT?

DON'T DODGE THE QUESTION!

WHAT DID HE GET YOU?

A PURPLE VESPA . . .

WHAT?!
Way to bury the lede!
That's so cool! You have to take me for a ride.

THE CRAZIEST THING HAPPENED AT R.O.A.R. PRACTICE TODAY.
WE WERE DOING SOME SWORD FIGHTING EXERCISES, BUT
THEN IT TURNED INTO THIS PRETTY INTENSE SPARRING
BATTLE BETWEEN ME AND THIS ONE OTHER KID. EVERYONE
WAS WATCHING.

SO FINALLY, I LEANED IN, USING THIS MOVE I USED A HUNDRED
TIMES ON THE ISLE. IT WORKS TO DISARM EVEN THE BEST
SWORDSMEN. BUT THEY BLOCKED IT AND JABBED BACK.
THIS WAS ONE OF THE BEST SWORDSMEN I'VE EVER FOUGHT
AGAINST. EXCEPT . . .

IT WASN'T A SWORDSMAN. IT WAS A SWORDS**WOMAN**.
IT WAS LONNIE! APPARENTLY SHE'S WANTED TO JOIN THE
TEAM FOR A WHILE NOW, AND SINCE BEN HAD TO DROP OUT
BECAUSE OF HIS KINGLY DUTIES, SHE FIGURED THERE WAS
A SPOT. BUT CHAD SAID THE RULES ARE THE RULES—THE
TEAM IS MADE UP OF THE CAPTAIN AND EIGHT MEN. I KNOW
COACH TRUSTED ME TO LEAD THE TEAM, AND I HAVE TO
FOLLOW THE RULES, BUT SHE *WAS SERIOUSLY GOOD.*

I WAS THERE! I SAW IT! WITH JUST A FLICK OF
HER WRIST, SHE TOSSED JAY'S SWORD ACROSS
THE FLOOR. IT WAS LIKE THREE SECONDS
BEFORE HE WAS TOTALLY DEFENSELESS.
HE DIDN'T STAND A CHANCE.

THANKS FOR REMINDING ME, CARLOS.

A Lady's Manners

Tips for Watching Fencing

1. Spectators are expected to stay in the background while the competitors fence.

2. At no time is one allowed to criticize the Officials or attempt to influence them in any way.

3. The best angle to watch a bout from is 45 degrees from the playing area.

I WONDER HOW ANNOYED LONNIE WOULD BE IF SHE SAW THIS

RULE #6 FROM THE R.O.A.R. RULE BOOK: A TEAM IS COMPOSED OF A <u>CAPTAIN</u> AND <u>EIGHT MEN.</u>

TOO BAD YOU CAN'T BREAK RULES IN AURADON. LONNIE WAS FIERCE.

111

ASKING JANE TO COTILLION, TAKE TWO

~~Black Cats~~
BROWN DOGS

SERIOUSLY. I TELL DUDE EVERYTHING. GLAD THE LITTLE MAN CAN KEEP A SECRET.

I SAW HER WALKING PAST R.O.A.R. PRACTICE TODAY, AND I RAN TO CATCH UP. SHE WAS TALKING ABOUT COTILLION AND ALL THE WORK SHE HAS TO DO FOR THE PLANNING COMMITTEE, SO IT SEEMED LIKE THE PERFECT TIME TO ASK HER. DUDE WAS RIGHT THERE, AND HE

There is no better companion
For a lonely witch or wizard
Than a ~~black cat,~~ BROWN DOG
Sly and agile,
~~A harbinger of bad luck~~
~~To all those who do not~~
~~conspire with its master.~~

STARTED WHINING TO GET ME TO SAY SOMETHING. BUT I DON'T KNOW . . . I JUST CHOKED. I COULDN'T DO IT. THEN SHE GOT THIS TEXT AND SAID SOMETHING ABOUT PARTY FAVORS, AND POOF! SHE WAS GONE.

I DON'T KNOW IF I'LL EVER FEEL BRAVE ENOUGH TO ASK HER. IT SEEMS LIKE JANE ONLY SEES ME AS A FRIEND, THAT'S IT. NOT A GUY SHE WOULD WANT TO GO OUT WITH. I SHOULD PROBABLY JUST GET USED TO THE IDEA OF GOING TO COTILLION ALONE.

Don't despair, Carlos. You can do it—I believe in you.
You just need to show her how you really feel.

HOW DO I GET OUT OF THE FRIEND ZONE?

-Dress to impress. Make sure you look handsome and sharp whenever you run into your crush. (Evie's 4 Hearts can help with this.)

-Be genuine and sweet.

-Work hard at school. Jane studies as much as I do, and she's going to want to be with someone who loves learning new things and has a passion for different subjects.

-Make a grand gesture. This can be bringing your crush flowers, making them a mix of songs you think they'd like, or asking them on a romantic horse-and-buggy ride.

-Show an interest in the things your crush is interested in. If she loves dancing, join the dance team.

BE YOURSELF. DON'T TRY TO BE SOMEONE YOU'RE NOT. IT'S REALLY IMPORTANT TO STAY TRUE TO YOURSELF, EVEN IF IT'S TEMPTING NOT TO.

-I THINK JUST SHOW YOUR CRUSH WHO YOU ARE. THAT'S THE HARDEST THING TO DO SOMETIMES.

-JUST. ASK. HER. OUT.

-DO. IT.

-STOP. BEING. SO. SCARED.

Truth Serum

PLEASE . . . I COULD REALLY USE THIS SERUM, WHETHER I'M PRETENDING OR NOT.

The TRUTH? Today I can barely breathe. THERE'S SO MUCH to do, and I've somehow only gotten around to doing half of it. WHEN I was IN THE middle of TRYING TO PLAN MY PICNIC WITH BEN, CARLOS TRACKED me down and said he needed a TRUTH SERUM so he could CONFESS his feelings for Jane. SURE, I KNOW THAT I'VE BEEN PRETENDING FOR THE last SIX MONTHS, RECITING SPELLS TO MAKE MY hair blonde and fit in like a TRUE lady, but I hope he doesn't follow MY example. Jane would be TOTALLY INTO him if he could just be himself.

Seekers of truth
will use this serum wisely.
Understanding it can
undo their enemies
Or birth surprising words
That otherwise would've
remained unsaid.

I should go. I have to TRACK down some GROUND PYTHON SKINS FOR THIS SPELL. I BROUGHT SOME FROM THE ISLE when I FIRST came HERE, but NOW I'M all out.

YOU KNOW I CAN READ, RIGHT?

If it is honesty you seek,

In a large selenite bowl

Mix one drop lobelia extract,

Two teaspoons ground python skins,

A large drop of spit, and one crow's foot.

Whisper the word "verum" three times.

As you dissolve a cup of sugar

into two spoonfuls red vinegar,

Let the mixture harden

into a sweet treat,

Making it palatable for consumption.

ARE YOU KIDDING ME?! YOU'RE GOING TO PUT YOUR SPIT IN THERE?

HOW'D YOU EVEN GET THAT? EWWWW!

I KNOW A GUY.

I was trying to get the last of the ingredients for Carlos's truth serum when Jane came up to me in the hall. I really like Jane and think she's sweet, but she's driving me a little bonkers with all these cotillion questions, like about the party favors. Apparently there are plastic hearts with a picture of Ben and me in them. Should they be charms or key chains or pen toppers?

It's not Jane's fault, but it just feels like all of this is so ... NOT ME. I used

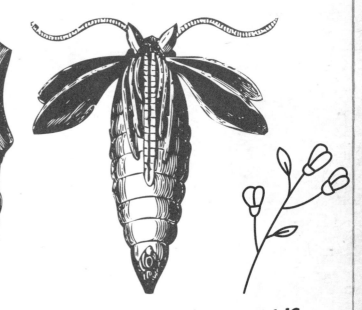

to love running around, snatching candy from kids, blasting music in our hideout so loud the neighbors would throw rocks through our windows. Now I'm the girl deciding between lilies and bluebells. When did I become someone who plans for a school dance months in advance?

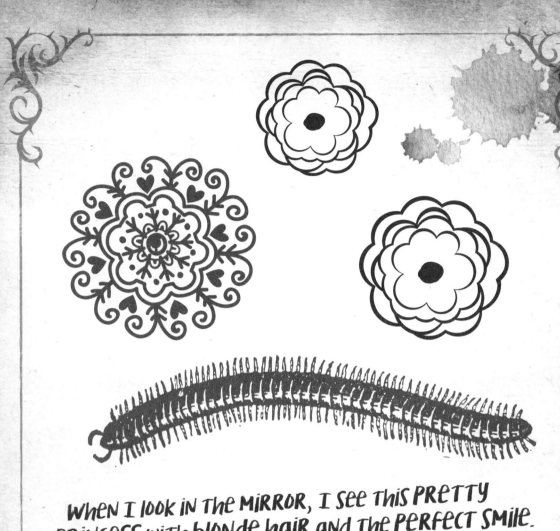

WHEN I look in THE MIRROR, I See THiS PRETTY PRINCESS WiTH blONDe hair and THE PERFECT SMile. She has GREAT MANNERS and everyone loves her FOR being So POLITE and So ladylike. She always SayS THE RIGHT THING AT THE RIGHT TIME and She NEVER Makes a MiSTAKE. EVER.

WHEN I look in THE MiRROR . . . I DON'T even RECOGNIZE MYSelf ANYMORE.

Fairy Wings

Fairy wings are inherited.
Stealing them or taking them by force
Can result in irreversible hexes
That one will never recover from.

If you are in want of a fairy wing,
It is wise to endear yourself to an elderly fairy,
One suffering from serious ailments,
One with no living kin,
One who is charmed by even your
most unfunny jokes.

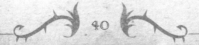

DOES ANYONE ELSE MISS THE ISLE OF THE LOST?
EVEN A TINY BIT?

SOMETIMES I have THE SUDDEN URGE TO RUN UP TO SOMEONE and SCREAM IN THEIR FACE, JUST TO SEE if I CAN SCARE THEM. OR GRAB all THE DESSERTS FROM THE DINING hall REFRIGERATOR and START a FOOD FIGHT. OR LIE TO SOMEONE JUST TO SEE if THEY'D BELIEVE ME.

Mal! You would get kicked out of Auradon Prep in a second. Can you imagine what would happen if you screamed in Belle's face?!

Stay close by her side
For fairy flights and tea
Until the time is right
To request the honor of her wings
Bequeathed to you after her passing.

I'M ROTTEN TO THE CORE
WHO COULD ask FOR MORE
I'M NOTHING like THE kid NEXT dOOR

... REMEMBER THAT?

MIGHT HAVE TO FIND ME A NICE OLD FAIRY. YOU NEVER KNOW WHEN A SET OF WINGS COULD COME IN HANDY!

THIS WHOLE COTILLION THING REALLY IS MAKING YOU CRAZY....

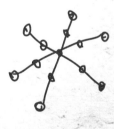

Ravens

The bird black as midnight,

With beady eyes, always searching:

He is the ultimate confidante.

Whispered words overheard by the raven

Will remain secret for centuries

Silencing all those with knowledge,

That might harm you.

Mal, maybe you should talk to Ben about what you're feeling.
I don't keep any secrets from Doug. Ben doesn't even know you're
using the spell book or that "Lady's Guide to Being Boring" book.

If he did, he'd probably tell you to stop.

HE WOULDN'T, THOUGH, EVIE. THAT'S THE POINT.
HE likes THE NEW Mal, THE ONE WITH blonde hair and
PERFECT MANNERS. All of AURADON does.

THEY THINK THAT'S WHO I AM.

SO TODAY MARKS THE THIRD TIME I CAUGHT CHAD SNEAKING INTO MY ROOM TO USE MY 3-D PRINTER. IT'S RIDICULOUS. BUT SOMEHOW, NO MATTER HOW MANY TIMES I IMAGINE TELLING HIM TO GET OUT OR GIVING HIM A WHOLE SPEECH ABOUT PRIVACY AND RESPECTING MY BOUNDARIES, I CAN'T ACTUALLY SAY IT ONCE HE'S THERE. I JUST LET HIM COME IN AND USE MY PRINTER LIKE IT'S HIS. AND THEN I FEEL TERRIBLE AFTER.

I FEEL LIKE EVERY TIME I DON'T SAY SOMETHING, I GET A LITTLE ANGRIER AT MYSELF.

DON'T GET MAD AT YOURSELF, CARLOS.
IT HAPPENS.
I DON'T HAVE ALL THE ANSWERS,
BUT I HOPE THIS HELPS. . . .

↓

HOW TO STAND UP TO SOMEONE

-BE CLEAR ABOUT WHAT YOU WANT. IF YOU DON'T WANT SOMEONE TALKING TO YOU ANYMORE, SAY THAT. IF YOU DON'T WANT THEM SNEAKING INTO YOUR ROOM ANYMORE AND USING YOUR 3-D PRINTER, SAY EXACTLY THAT.

-IF THE PERSON IGNORES YOU, BE CLEAR __AGAIN__ ABOUT WHAT YOU WANT. DON'T LET THEM PRETEND THEY DIDN'T HEAR WHAT YOU SAID.

-IF THE PERSON STILL TRIES TO IGNORE YOU, TAKE ACTION TO MAKE THEM LISTEN. MAYBE THAT MEANS CHANGING THE LOCKS ON YOUR DOOR. OR MAYBE THAT MEANS HIDING YOUR PRINTER SO THEY CAN'T USE IT WHENEVER THEY WANT.

-NEVER LET SOMEONE MAKE YOU FEEL LIKE THAT. SERIOUSLY—YOU'RE ONE OF MY FAVORITE PEOPLE, CARLOS.

I WONDER IF THIS COULD WORK FOR THE R.O.A.R. TEAM.
WOULDN'T HURT TO HAVE A LITTLE PROTECTION SPELL
BEFORE A MATCH, RIGHT? MAL?

A Spell for Protection

A hex, a curse,

A severed bat head in your purse . . .

Whatever evil your enemy has in Store,

This protective Spell is the perfect cure.

CAN'T HELP YOU, JAY.
I SHOULDN'T EVEN
BE USING ANY OF THE
SPELLS IN THIS BOOK.

CHAD CAME IN TO
USE MY 3-D
PRINTER AGAIN,
AND THIS TIME HE
PRINTED HIS OWN
KEY SO HE COULD
COME AND GO AS
HE PLEASED. I DID
EXACTLY WHAT YOU SAID,
JAY, AND IT TOTALLY WORKED. HE LEFT THE KEY ON
MY DESK AND WALKED OUT THE DOOR.

I THINK HE'S JUST FEELING A LITTLE LOST LATELY. HE'S BEEN CLINGY SINCE AUDREY'S BEEN AWAY. THE GUY DOESN'T HAVE A TON OF PEOPLE TO HANG OUT WITH, AND HE SEEMED GENUINELY BUMMED OUT WHEN JAY WAS MADE CAPTAIN OF THE R.O.A.R. TEAM INSTEAD OF HIM. BUT ANYWAY . . . I'M FORGETTING THE CRAZIEST PART OF THE STORY. MAL WAS THERE TO GIVE ME THE TRUTH SERUM, WHICH SHE MADE INTO A CHERRY GUMDROP. SHE WAS HOLDING IT BEHIND HER BACK, GIVING ME THIS SPEECH ABOUT TELLING THE TRUTH, AND HOW MAYBE IT'S NOT ALWAYS THE BEST THING TO DO, WHEN DUDE RAN OVER TO HER AND ATE IT OUT OF HER HAND. WITHIN SECONDS, HE WAS TALKING.

In a scrying bowl place a rare, precious stone of amethyst, schorl, or malachite. Recite these words on the third Sunday of the month When the sun has just touched the horizon:

<u>NOW I HAVE A TALKING DOG.</u>

HE WAS LITERALLY JUST TELLING ME TO SCRATCH HIS BUTT. MAL DIDN'T HAVE TIME TO MAKE AN ANTIDOTE, WHICH HONESTLY I'M FINE WITH.

HOW COOL IS THIS?!

WHAAAAAT?! I need to see this ASAP!

IT'S KIND OF AWESOME.

Give this Stone the Strength of protection.

May anyone who nears it be purified,

Their ill intentions transformed

To those of kindness and goodwill.

Wear the protective Stone for

one hundred and seven days

Hanging from a Strip of <u>toad leather</u>,

Resting safely against your heart.

SAVE THE TOADS

THIS IS SERIOUSLY GROSS. YOU TWO ARE GOING TO CHOP UP A TOAD AND USE ITS SKIN? WHAT KIND OF MONSTERS ARE YOU?

RELAX! I MISSED THIS PART—I DIDN'T EVEN REALIZE IT WAS PART OF THE PROTECTION SPELL!

A Lady in Conversation

A lady never raises her voice.

A lady never uses bad words.

A lady never laughs too loudly.

A lady never stands too close to whomever she's talking to.

A lady never yawns. **BUT SOMETIMES I'M TIRED!**

A lady never gossips. **GOSSIPING WAS MY FAVORITE PASTIME ON THE ISLE....**

A lady never corrects someone's grammar.

A lady knows that a person's name is music to them.

A lady never forgets a name. **I'VE DEFINITELY FORGOTTEN SOME NAMES THESE PAST MONTHS.**

A lady knows many different topics for polite conversation.

A lady knows how to say "please" and "thank you."

A lady knows how to accept a compliment.

I WOULD NEVER. NO, SERIOUSLY, I WOULD NEVER DO THIS. EVER.

Okay, maybe I miss gossip a tiny bit.
Remember when Harry Hook fell into a barrel of
rotting fish? He smelled like guts for weeks.

HOW COULD I FORGET?

WHAT I MiSS MOST about the ISLe of THe LOST

- DOing WHATEVER I WANT WHENEVER I WANT
  - NOT LiSTENING TO ANYONE
- MY hideOUT
  - RUNNING WiLD IN THE STREETS
  - HAVING NO RULES
  - HAVING NO RESPONSIBILITIES
- NOT WORRYING About FITTING IN
  - NOT WORRYING About PEOPLE LIKING ME
  - NOT WORRYING

That place was pretty great. But I guess what I miss most is hanging out with you there, and we can still do that in Auradon.

FINE. YOU GOT ME—I DO MISS THAT, TOO. I CAN'T REMEMBER THE LAST TIME I SCREAMED.

I DO. LAST NIGHT. WHEN YOU STUBBED YOUR TOE ON YOUR DESK.

I MEANT FOR FUN. DUH.

Beware Enchanted Lakes

Witches and warlocks, beware:
There is a formidable foe
Stronger than your strongest enemy.

Swimming in an enchanted lake
Can leach your power
And tear down your defenses,
Reversing all spells that have been cast.

Oh, no. I didn't even see this until now. . . .
I'm glad I haven't gone swimming in there—
it would've changed my hair back to purple.

Reversal Spell for a Feast

Take this feast, this sumptuous meal,

Return it back to what was real.

Today was the WORST. I JUST left BEN at the ENCHANTED Lake and I'M SITTING IN THE WOODS, TRYING TO avoid EVERYONE I'VE EVER MET. I feel SO lost. And FRUSTRATED. And ANGRY and EMBARRASSED. I DON'T EVEN KNOW WHERE TO START. . . .

I SPENT THE WHOLE AFTERNOON MAKING THAT TRUTH SERUM FOR CARLOS, and THEN DUDE gobbled IT DOWN. I DIDN'T have ANY TIME TO MAKE AN ANTIDOTE, SO NOW THERE'S a TALKING dOG RUNNING around AURADON, ASKING PEOPLE TO RUB HIS TUMMY. THERE WAS NO TIME TO WORRY ABOUT THAT, THOUGH, because I had TO MEET BEN FOR OUR SPECIAL PICNIC date.

I WENT DOWN TO THE ENCHANTED LAKE EARLY SO
THAT I WOULD BE BACK IN TIME FOR MY FITTING WITH
EVIE. I BROUGHT ALL THE FOODS I'D MADE WITH THE
FEAST SPELL, AND THE PICNIC BASKET AND BLANKET
AND ALL THE SPECIAL SILVERWARE AND PLATES I'D
BORROWED FROM THE COTILLION PLANNING COMMITTEE.
(I EVEN REMEMBERED THE DESSERT SPOONS. WIN.)

AS SOON AS BEN ARRIVED,
IT FELT LIKE IT WAS ALL
WORTH IT. HE WAS SO
IMPRESSED WITH
EVERYTHING I'D
DONE.
I'D
TURNED
THE OLD
COOKIE
AND THE
SANDWICH INTO
THE FEAST
MRS. POTTS MADE FOR
HIS PARENTS. FOR THAT ONE MOMENT, LOOKING INTO
HIS EYES, I FELT CALM. HAPPY. IT SEEMED LIKE ALL THE
COTILLION CHAOS WAS FAR AWAY, IN SOME OTHER WORLD.

Rat Skulls

My hex days ARE OVER ____
That's one spell I'll NEVER go back to.

A rat skull is a particularly useful
Ingredient in Spell casting.
In powder form it can Strengthen hexes.

For best results, grind the skull
With a mortar and pestle made of black granite,
Mix in a single wizard's tear,
And Store in the darkest dungeon,
Letting the powder age for thirteen days.

BUT THEN BEN leaned over and noticed my spell book was tucked away in the picnic basket. Before I could STOP him, he pulled it out and started flipping through it. He stopped on some pretty incriminating spells. The feast spell. The blonde hair spell. Within seconds, I confessed everything: how I'd been using the spells to fit in. How hard it all had been.

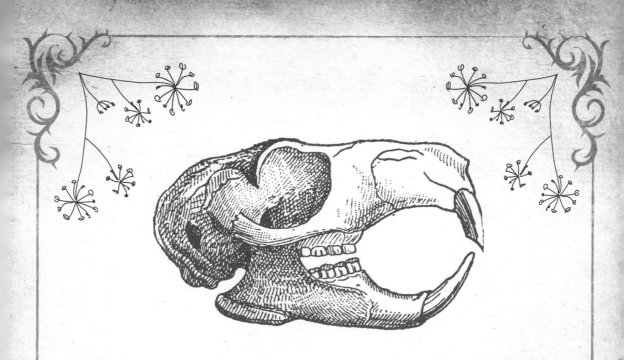

He felt so betrayed. I'll never forget that look in his eyes as he stared down at the spell book, realizing the last few months I'd been lying to him. "you've been keeping secrets and lying. Again," he said. "This isn't the Isle of the Lost, Mal."

He kind of hit the nail on the head: Auradon definitely isn't the Isle of the Lost. I'll never feel at home here the way I did on the Isle. I'll always have to think before I speak, before I act, before I do anything. I don't belong here. Ben is a perfect king, and everyone expects him to be with a perfect lady.

That's not what I am. I'm a villain kid from the Isle of the Lost. I've got wicked running through my veins.

STAYING IN AURADON

PROS
- I GET TO BE WITH BEN.
  - I DON'T HAVE TO LEAVE EVIE, JAY, AND CARLOS.
- THERE ARE SO MANY OPPORTUNITIES HERE.

CONS
- I have to deal with CAMERAS and PAPARAZZI.
  - IT will NEVER feel like home.
- I have to TRY so hard.
- I hate following all THE RULES FROM <u>A LADY'S MANNERS.</u>
  - I DON'T KNOW if I WANT TO be lady of THE COURT.
- EVERYONE is watching ME all THE TIME.
  - MY whole life is MAPPED OUT FOR ME here.

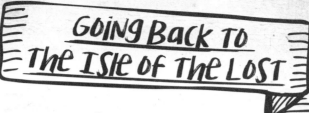

GOING BACK TO THE ISLE OF THE LOST

PROS

- IT FEELS LIKE HOME.
  - I CAN BE MYSELF THERE.
- I WOULDN'T HAVE TO PRETEND ANYMORE.
  - NO CAMERAS, NO ONE WATCHING ME
- REAL FREEDOM
  - NO RULES
- PRIVACY

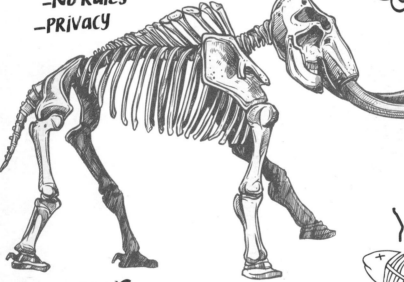

CONS

- I'll MISS BEN. (BUT does he love who I REALLY am?)
- I'll MISS MY FRIENDS.
  - I do have SOME enemies on THE ISLE.
- NO MAGIC

Magical Transport Spell

An Egyptian rug,

Rolled up in the corner;

A broken bicycle,

Its tires flattened and bent;

An old dusty broom;

A plump little pumpkin,

Or a dragon, flared nostrils and fiery breath . . .

SOMETHING HAS CHANGED. I JUST GOT BACK TO MY ROOM, AND EVIE ISN'T HERE. IT'S WEIRDLY QUIET. MY MOM IS PEERING AT ME FROM HER CAGE, AND IT FEELS LIKE FOR THE FIRST TIME IN A LONG TIME, I'M REALLY SEEING HER. AND I'M REMEMBERING WHO I AM AND WHERE I'M FROM. I DON'T BELONG HERE, AND SHE DOESN'T BELONG HERE, EITHER. MAYBE IT ISN'T "GOOD" OR THE RIGHT THING TO DO, BUT I CAN'T BE SOMEONE I'M NOT. I DON'T WANT TO PRETEND ANYMORE. WE'RE GOING HOME.

LET'S HOPE THIS INCLUDES VESPAS . . . .

Any object or creature will do.
Just say these words to transport you:

Noble Steed, proud and fair,
You shall take me anywhere.

I should've used these more to hide from paparazzi.

Disguises and Deceptions

It is an invaluable skill
To be able to change your appearance
As fast as the crow flies south.

Peruse these spells and incantations
To discover the perfect disguise
For any misdeeds you may be plotting.

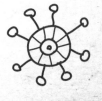

The Mustachioed Man

Hair as thick as yarn
Sprouting from the barren skin
Above your sneering lips,
Twisting and curling at its ends,
A caterpillar-like thing
Perfect to deceive
Even the most perceptive foes . . .

I'M WRITING THIS FROM HIGH ABOVE THE ISLE STREETS, BACK IN MY HIDEOUT. IT FEELS SO GOOD TO BE HERE, SURROUNDED BY ALL MY FAMILIAR THINGS. THE GRAFFITI MURAL EVIE AND I MADE ONE DAY WHEN WE WERE BORED. MY PURPLE SLEEPING BAG THAT STILL SMELLS A LITTLE MUSTY—BUT GOOD MUSTY, LIKE YOUR BEST FRIEND'S DUNGEON. AND MY FAVORITE COUCH IN THE WHOLE WORLD, WHICH IS SO MUSHY THAT WHEN YOU SIT IN IT, YOUR WHOLE BODY SINKS AND IT FEELS LIKE IT'S GIVING YOU A HUG. I'VE SLEPT THERE FOR DAYS.

AFTER I LEFT THE DORMS, I TOOK MY VESPA THROUGH THE CITY AND DOWN TO BELLE'S HARBOR. I JUST SAT THERE, STARING OUT OVER THE WATER AT THE ISLE OF THE LOST, WONDERING IF I COULD REALLY DO IT. IF I'D REALLY BREAK THE BARRIER AND GO BACK. BEFORE I COULD SECOND-GUESS MYSELF, I RECITED THE SPELL AND WAS FLYING. UP, OVER THE WATER AND TOWARD THE BARRIER. WITHIN SECONDS I HAD BROKEN THROUGH.

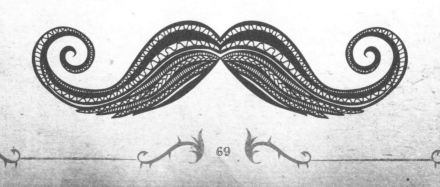

To grow a luscious mustache,

Procure a brass cauldron

From a young witch's lair.

In it, combine a fistful of newt eyes,

One cup of stallion's blood,

And a single hair from the head of a giant.

Let simmer for twelve hours

Over a fire built from hemlock branches,

Then set aside to cool.

Smear above your top lip as you incant:

AS SOON AS I TOUCHED DOWN ON THE ISLE, PEOPLE STARTED TO RECOGNIZE ME.

Mal, THE TRAITOR.

Mal, THE GOODY TWO-SHOES, SOON-TO-BE lady of THE COURT.

I ZIPPED PAST AND SOME OF THEM POINTED AND GRABBED THEIR FRIENDS. I GUESS THEY'VE BEEN WATCHING FOOTAGE FROM AURADON AND HAVE SEEN ALL THE CLIPS OF ME AND BEN. THEY PROBABLY HEARD ABOUT MY MOM TURNING INTO A LIZARD, TOO.

A wild mustache, bushy and thick—
Grow it now, grow it quick.
Give me a look no one will recognize:
Coarse black* hair, what a cunning disguise.

*May be replaced with blonde, gray,
white, blue, purple, or red

IT was different from the way people looked at me in AURADON, but I liked it. They were looking at all of me— the good and the bad—and NOT JUST the PERFECT lady I was PRETENDING to be. I WASN'T hiding ANYMORE. I was JUST ME.

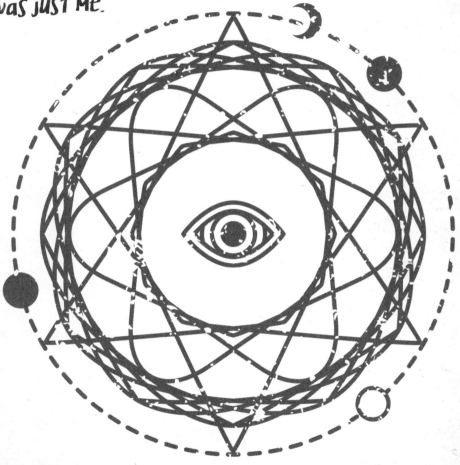

MY FAVORITE THINGS ABOUT THE HIDEOUT

- The candy Evie and I hid in an old box under the couch

- My <u>long live evil</u> t-shirt, which is so worn out it's really soft

- The way it always smells a little like burnt garbage and sour milk—GROSS but COMFORTING

- The call horn where people can ask to come up

- The place underneath the table where Jay, Carlos, Evie, and I carved our names

- The view of all the dirty streets and alleys

- Throwing things at the street sign to open the gate

Blonde Hair Spell

A princess with a pure heart
Often possesses hair of gold,
The color of the sun
When it first appears in the sky.

If it is blonde hair you yearn for,
In a large bronze cauldron
Combine two teaspoons fairy dust,
One minced sparrow spleen,
And a gallon of water
From a river on a line of power.
Submerge your locks in the solution
As you incant:

With these gorgeous locks so fair,
Turn them gold and light as air.

Make it blonde and full like thunder
So everyone will stare in wonder.

Stack it high upon my crown,
That I should never
let it down!

I FORGOT TO MENTION . . . I left BEN'S RING IN MY DORM ROOM. I TOOK MY MOM'S DRAGON RING WITH ME INSTEAD. IT JUST SEEMED TOO SAD TO BRING BEN'S RING TO THE ISLE. EVERY TIME I LOOKED AT IT, I WOULD'VE JUST GOTTEN UPSET AND THEN STARTED TO MISS HIM AND THEN QUESTIONED MY DECISION. THIS IS WHAT I NEEDED TO DO.

THIS IS WHAT'S RIGHT.

I JUST GOT BACK FROM LADY TREMAINE'S CURL UP AND
DYE SALON. I WAS DESPERATE TO GET BACK MY OLD LOOK.

WHEN I PEERED INSIDE, I WAS RELIEVED TO SEE DIZZY,
LADY TREMAINE'S GRANDDAUGHTER. LADY TREMAINE
WASN'T THERE, BUT APPARENTLY SHE HAS GONE FROM
EVIL STEPMOTHER TO EVIL GRANDMOTHER. SHE HAS
DIZZY SWEEPING AND SCOURING ALL DAY, EVEN THOUGH
DIZZY IS DYING (PUN INTENDED) TO TAKE ON CLIENTS
OF HER OWN. I DON'T TRUST JUST ANYONE WITH MY
hair, BUT EVIE AND DIZZY WERE GOOD FRIENDS
WHEN WE WERE ON THE ISLE, and

EVIE
WAS ALWAYS
RAVING ABOUT WHAT GREAT STYLE DIZZY had. I DIDN'T
have EVIE THERE TO help GET ME back TO MY OLD
look, BUT I FIGURED DIZZY would be a PRETTY good
SUBSTITUTE STYLIST.

I GOT MY hair DYED and MY NAILS POLISHED—I'M back
TO NORMAL. I FEEL BETTER THAN I have IN WEEKS.
MY hair IS PURPLE, and DIZZY gave ME dARK NAIL POLISH,
which I HAVEN'T had IN MONTHS. I have TO TELL YOU

THE CRAZIEST THING THAT HAPPENED THERE,
BUT I'M SO TIRED MY EYES ARE FALLING SHUT.
I THINK THAT MAGICAL TRANSPORT SPELL TOOK
A LOT OUT OF ME.

TO BE CONTINUED . . .

A ~~Princess~~ VILLAIN So Pretty

An essential spell
For any witch or warlock
With gnarled hands,
A wrinkled, pockmarked face,
Or rotten teeth . . .

Transform into a princess
Prized for beauty,
Beloved by all,
And deceive even the most
Discerning prince.

I'M DONE WITH PRETENDING.
IT'S SO MUCH EASIER TO JUST BE YOURSELF.

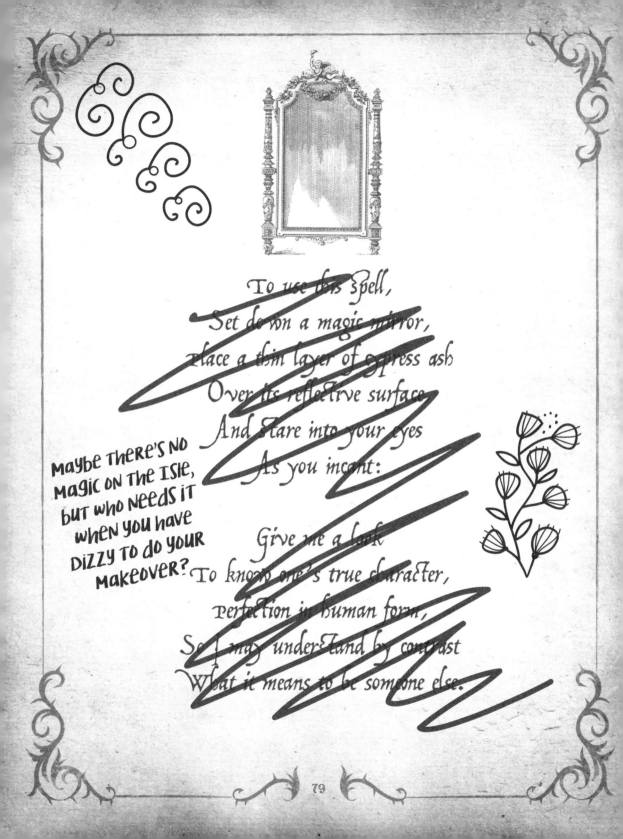

To use this spell,
Set down a magic mirror,
Place a thin layer of cypress ash
Over its reflective surface,
And stare into your eyes
As you incant:

Give me a look
To know one's true character,
Perfection in human form,
So I may understand by contrast
What it means to be someone else.

Maybe there's no magic on the Isle, but who needs it when you have Dizzy to do your makeover?

ISLE OF THE LOST BEAUTY TIPS

(FROM MY NEW STYLIST, DIZZY)

-A villain kid always has her hair cut with garden shears.

-A villain kid always has her hair ironed with an old-fashioned iron.

-A villain kid knows the best way to create volume is to set his or her hair with soda can rollers. Dented old cans are perfectly okay.

-A villain kid lets her stylist use a curling iron on her hair, even if she sees that it's rusty. Nothing creates an edgy hairstyle like a rusty curling iron.

-A villain kid knows that sewer sludge is the best way to remove cuticles. She submerges her hands in sludge, preferably hot and bubbling, before every manicure.

WHAT I'LL MISS MOST

I'll miss the way Ben looked at me.
The way he touched my cheek.
How it felt when we held hands.
His kindness.

I'll miss the way Evie and I laughed together.

How sometimes she could tell what I was thinking without me having to say a word.

All the beautiful clothes she made me, and how much thought and care she put into every piece. (I don't think I'll ever meet another person as talented as Evie.)

Staying up late, talking.

I'll miss everything about her.

I'll miss my one true friend.

I'll miss hanging out in the courtyard with Carlos, playing fetch with Dude.

How you can say anything to him and he'll understand. He's a great listener.

His sweetness.

I'll miss having Jay as a big brother. Knowing he always has my back, no matter what.

How he teased me.

How he always made me laugh.

How sometimes I'd catch him looking in the mirror, making a muscle, and we'd crack up.

His loyalty.

A Giant's Height

A low vantage point
May not be desirable
For the villain
Who seeks unrelenting power.

To gain the height you require,
Stand at the shore of an enchanted lake
With a talisman of alexandrite
And recite these words:

WHERE WAS I? Oh... THE CRAZY THING THAT HAPPENED
AT LADY TREMAINE'S SHOP. DIZZY HAD JUST FINISHED UP MY
MAKEOVER. I'D GIVEN HER A TIP TO THANK HER, WHICH SHE
SEEMED TOTALLY SURPRISED BY. (THAT MADE ME REALLY SAD.
SHE DESERVED IT AND THEN SOME, BUT IT WAS CLEAR NO ONE
HAD EVER ACTUALLY PAID HER.)

A giant's build,
Fearsome and tall,
Let me rise ten* inches
To amaze and appall.

*May be replaced with any number
of inches one wishes to grow

THEN I HEARD THE DOOR OPEN, AND I TURNED AND SAW
HARRY, CAPTAIN HOOK'S SON. HE STOLE EVERYTHING FROM
DIZZY'S CASH REGISTER. I'VE SEEN ROBBERIES HUNDREDS
OF TIMES ON THE ISLE, BUT IT STILL BOTHERED ME. SOMETHING
LIKE THAT WOULD NEVER HAPPEN IN AURADON.

That makes me so sad. Poor Dizzy.

The Best Ways to Poison a Princess

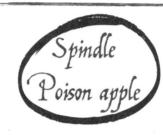

Spindle
Poison apple

MY MOM and EVIE'S MOM USED TO ARGUE FOR DAYS ABOUT THIS. LITERALLY.

I hadN'T SEEN HARRY IN a while. He'S ONE OF UMA'S MINIONS, RUNNING AROUND aND THREATENING KIDS ON HER BEHALF. He DOES EVERYTHING SHE SAYS, SO MUCH THAT I'M NOT COMPLETELY SURE he has his OWN BRAIN. OR IF He DOES, IT DEFINITELY DOESN'T WORK.

UMA, URSULA'S DAUGHTER. SHE aND I have BEEN FIGHTING SINCE WE WERE KIDS. SHE RUNS HER MOTHER'S FISH aND CHIPS SHOPPE, aND HARRY INFORMED ME THAT SINCE I LEFT THE ISLE, SHE'S TAKEN OVER MY TERRITORY. I INFORMED HIM THAT WHATEVER happened while I WaS gone WaS ONLY TEMPORARY. I'M BACK NOW, aND a VILLAIN KID ISN'T a VILLAIN WITHOUT HER OWN TURF.

I HOPE THINGS DON'T have TO GET UGLY....

FACING OFF AGAINST AN OPPONENT

-A villain kid always stands up for herself.

-A villain kid NEVER gives up her TERRITORY.

-A villain kid NEVER lets anyone tell her what's what.

-A villain kid isn't afraid to raise her voice.

-A villain kid isn't scared of anyone or anything. **YES! VK FOR LIFE!**

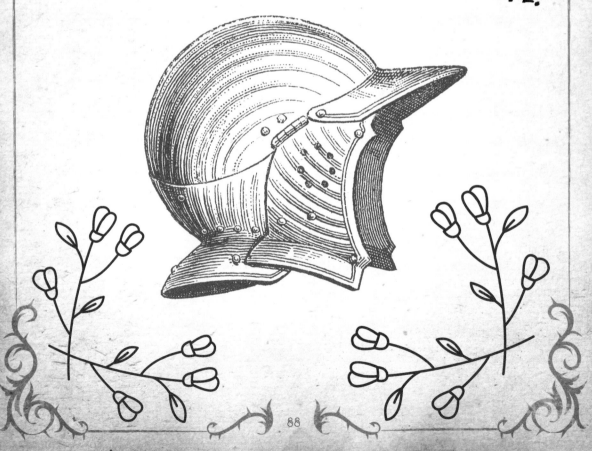

I'LL NEVER STOP BEING A VILLAIN KID.

As much as I love Auradon, this list really does remind me what makes us so great. My VK pride is a real thing. I'll never lose that.

How to Charm a Snake

Possessing the mind of a serpent
Is an invaluable skill
For any witch or warlock
Who yearns for unrelenting power.

Pythons, cobras, and yellow vipers
Are all fine servants
With sharp fangs,
Slithering tongues, and
Constricting, twisted tails.

To harness these creatures
Of sand and rock and tree limb,
Stare into their eyes,
Black as a raven's wing,
And recite the following:

Serpentine Stranger,
We now are joined for the ages.
Go forth and do my bidding.

Amber

Amber is known for its healing properties,
Providing clarity of thought
And a release from physical pain.
Amulets with a spider
Trapped and fossilized inside
Are said to possess strong magic
And the ability to repel enemies.

AMBER MIGHT be GOOD NOW THAT I'M back ON THE
ISLe. I ShOULD TRY TO TRACK DOWN a PieCe. . . . .

TODAY I GOT back TO IT. TOOK OUT MY OLD SPRAY PAINTS
AND STARTED A MURAL ON THE HIDEOUT WALL. IT FELT
GOOD TO be HeRe again, alONe, PAINTING LIKE I USED TO.
I GOT SO absORbed IN THe MURAL IT TOOK Me A SeCOND
TO NOTICE BEN had FOUND Me.

HE CAME ALL THE WAY FROM AURADON WITH EVIE, JAY, LONNIE, AND CARLOS. HE WANTED ME TO GO BACK WITH HIM. HE JUST STOOD THERE IN THE DOORWAY, HOLDING OUT HIS RING, WAITING FOR ME TO TAKE IT. AND THEN HE SAID IT: "DON'T QUIT US, MAL. THE PEOPLE LOVE YOU. <u>I LOVE YOU</u>."

AFTER, THERE WAS SILENCE. SO MUCH SILENCE. I KNOW I WAS SUPPOSED TO SAY THAT I LOVED HIM, TOO, BUT I COULDN'T. NOT NOW. I HAVE TO TAKE MYSELF OUT OF THE EQUATION. IT'S WHAT'S BEST FOR ME, AND IT'S WHAT'S BEST FOR AURADON. IF I WENT BACK, IT WOULD ONLY BE A MATTER OF TIME BEFORE I SLIPPED UP AND DID SOMETHING TO EMBARRASS MYSELF AND BEN. I CAN'T TAKE THAT CHANCE.

IT MUST'VE CRUSHED HIM, WAITING THERE FOR ME TO SAY IT BACK. IT FELT LIKE TEN YEARS WENT BY IN THOSE FEW SECONDS. THEN HE JUST LEFT.

I KNOW IT WAS THE RIGHT THING TO DO, BUT I FEEL MORE ALONE THAN EVER. . . . .

A Spell for New Beginnings ♡

How weary is the soul of the eternal traveler
Who has loved with a fiery passion and met heartbreak,
Who has built his castle and suffered a siege,
Who has lost battles and countries and kinsmen,
Who has rested and healed
Only to be struck down again?

I have to say good-bye to Auradon. No matter what happened there, no matter how great it was, I have to let it go.

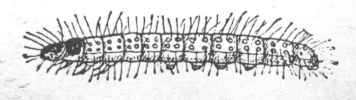

AFTER BEN LEFT, EVIE TRIED TO CALL TO ME ON THE HIDEOUT INTERCOM. I TOLD THEM, TO GO AWAY—THE SOUND OF HER VOICE WAS TOO MUCH TO TAKE. I NEVER ASKED THEM TO COME HERE. I'M NOT SOME PRINCESS IN A TOWER AND I CERTAINLY DON'T NEED TO BE RESCUED. AND NO MATTER HOW MUCH I WANT TO GO BACK, OR WANT TO BE WITH MY FRIENDS, IT'S JUST NOT THAT SIMPLE.
NOTHING IS ANYMORE.

Again and again
He falls, but he must fear not,
For new beginnings are nigh.

On the last moon before the fullest,
Stand on the banks of an enchanted lake,
Open your arms to the sky,
And repeat these words three times:

Gone is the past,
Released into the cosmos,
Burning bright above.
May the fire of the stars release me.
May the planets prepare me
For new beginnings to wonder and delight.

I kept painting, losing myself as I finished the mural. I don't know how much time passed, but at some point, Jay, Carlos and Evie came to see me. I was about to tell them exactly what I told Ben, that I wasn't going anywhere.

But that's not why they were here. "Ben's been captured," they told me. "We need you."

I knew we were in trouble the minute we stepped out of the limo. I could dress Ben in VK clothes, and put a hat on him, and style his hair, but there was no way he was ever going to fit in here. When we walked down the street, Ben kept saying "please" and "thank you" to people. He was waving and smiling at them.

Word must've spread quickly that we were here....

DIDN'T HE SHAKE SOMEONE'S HAND? SO EMBARRASSING.

A LITTLE RESPECT, GUYS. HE COULD BE IN SERIOUS TROUBLE.

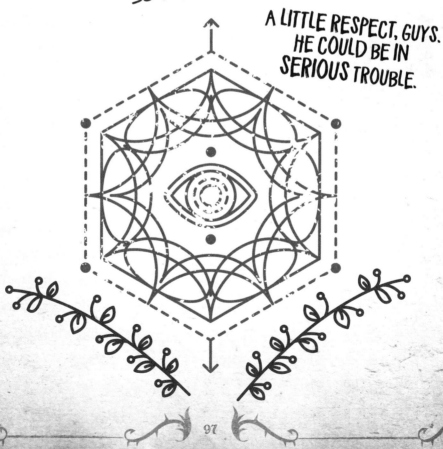

Incantation for Wealth

Rubies, diamonds, sapphires, and gold
Emerald rings to be bought or sold
The world will give you the wealth you desire
If you recite these words over a goblin's fire:

Send me a treasure to survive the ages
Summon it forth from these tattered pages

THAT HAPPENED REALLY FAST. I KEEP RUNNING
THROUGH IT IN MY MIND, TRYING TO FIGURE OUT IF I
MISSED ANY CLUES. BEN CLIMBED DOWN FROM THE
HIDEOUT AND TOLD US MAL DIDN'T WANT TO COME
BACK TO AURADON. HE LOOKED LIKE SOMEONE HAD JUST
PUNCHED HIM IN THE STOMACH, AND HE WALKED OFF
UNDER THE BRIDGE. I DIDN'T THINK HE WAS GOING FAR.

EVIE STARTED CALLING UP TO MAL ON THE INTERCOM, BUT THAT DIDN'T WORK. THEN JAY SAID SOMETHING ABOUT GIVING MAL SOME TIME TO COOL OFF, AND THAT'S WHEN I TURNED AROUND.

IT COULDN'T HAVE BEEN MORE THAN A MINUTE. THAT'S ALL IT TOOK FOR THEM TO CAPTURE BEN.

Harry Hook. What a wharf rat! I had forgotten how much I despised him, but then I saw him sneering at me from the shadows. I hated the way he smiled at us when he said it. "We nicked Ben," he said. "And if you want to see him again, have Mal come to the chip shop tonight. Alone. Uma wants a little visit."

The only person as bad as Harry Hook is Gil, Gaston's son. And the only person worse than the two of them combined is Uma.

Wow, it is so awful to be back.

Home, Wretched Home

Worst Things About Harry Hook

-How he always smells like rotting fish guts

-How he picks his teeth with his hook

-How he can't think for himself

-How he curls his lip in that gross little sneer

HE SAID I'VE LOST MY EDGE.

HOW. DARE. HE.

Baby Spiders

Baby spiders are a delicacy
That complement any dish.
They are best served
Just minutes after hatching
On a stale baguette
With day-old fish guts.

A lady never arm
wrestles in public.
(Kidding!)

MY ARM IS STILL SORE. I WENT TO URSULA'S FISH & CHIPS SHOP,
ALONE, JUST LIKE UMA ASKED ME TO. JAY, CARLOS, AND EVIE
had WANTED TO COME AS BACKUP, BUT I KNOW THAT'S NOT
WHAT THIS IS ABOUT. UMA AND I have BEEN FEUDING SINCE . . .
. WELL, FOREVER. I USED TO CALL HER SHRIMPY AND SOMEHOW,
all THESE YEARS LATER, SHE STILL HASN'T GOTTEN OVER IT.
IT SEEMS LIKE EVERYONE ON THE ISLE IS ANGRY I WENT FROM
BEING BAD TO GOOD.

I STROLLED INTO THE PLACE, ACTING LIKE IT WAS MY SHOP, SOMEWHERE I HUNG OUT EVERY DAY FOR THE PAST YEAR. IF I KNOW ANYTHING ABOUT UMA, IT'S THAT SHE RELISHES SCARING PEOPLE. MAKING THEM UNCOMFORTABLE. INTIMIDATING THEM. I DIDN'T WANT TO GIVE HER EVEN THE TINIEST BIT OF SATISFACTION. SHE STARTED BABBLING, SOMETHING ABOUT WATCHING ME SQUIRM LIKE A WORM ON A HOOK, BUT I JUST SHRUGGED IT OFF. "IF YOU HAVE A SCORE TO SETTLE WITH ME, BRING IT," I SAID. "NO NEED TO DRAG IN BEN."

SHE PROPOSED AN ARM WRESTLING MATCH, PROBABLY BECAUSE SHE WANTED TO CREATE A SPECTACLE FOR ALL THE SORRY PEOPLE WHO WERE EATING (OR NOT EATING . . . JUST STARING AT THEIR NASTY FOOD) IN HER SHOP. SHE SAID IF I WON, BEN WOULD GO FREE. THEN, IN THE MIDDLE OF THE MATCH, SHE SAID IF SHE WON, I'D HAVE TO BRING HER FAIRY GODMOTHER'S WAND. I DON'T KNOW WHAT HAPPENED—I MUST'VE LOST MY CONCENTRATION WHEN SHE SAID IT. MY ELBOW MUST'VE SLIPPED. ALL I KNOW IS THAT WITHIN SECONDS, THE BACK OF MY HAND HIT THE TABLE. OR THE SCALLYWAG CHEATED. I DON'T TRUST ANYTHING SHE SAYS OR DOES.

I CAN'T BELIEVE I LET HER PLAY ME LIKE THAT. I GUESS BEING IN AURADON ALL THAT TIME MADE ME A LITTLE SOFT. BUT NOT FOR LONG.

"BRING IT TO MY SHIP TOMORROW AT NOON," SHE SAID. "IF YOU BLAB, YOU CAN KISS YOUR BABY GOOD-BYE."

YOU'RE MISSING THE CRAZIEST PART. HOW ARE WE GOING TO GET FAIRY GODMOTHER'S MAGIC WAND? AND HOW CAN WE GIVE IT TO UMA?! SHE'S GOING TO DESTROY ALL OF AURADON.

The Autumn Equinox

On this day in September
The sun crosses the celestial equator,
And in these long hours sunlight will match darkness.

Equinoxes are perfect times
For spell casting and conjuring.
Protection spells work best
When incanted at sunset,
And reversal spells can be strengthened
If recited in the moment
Of the sun's equatorial crossing.

THE PLAN

1. CARLOS AND I WILL TAKE THE LIMO BACK TO AURADON.

2. CARLOS WILL PRINT A FAKE MAGIC WAND ON HIS 3-D PRINTER.

3. MAL AND EVIE WILL GO TO LADY TREMAINE'S SHOP TO MAKE SMOKE BOMBS.

4. WE'LL MEET BACK UP AT THE DOCKS TOMORROW, JUST BEFORE NOON.

5. DELIVER THE FAKE MAGIC WAND TO UMA.

6. GET BEN BACK.

7. USE THE SMOKE BOMBS AS A DISTRACTION TO GET AWAY.

8. GET BACK TO AURADON ASAP.

I CAN'T WAIT TO SEE UMA'S FACE WHEN SHE REALIZES THE WAND'S FAKE....

This _has_ to work!!

OKAY, JAY AND I ARE HEADING OUT NOW TO GO BACK TO AURADON. WE WILL SEE YOU BOTH TOMORROW DOWN BY THE DOCK, RIGHT BEFORE WE GIVE UMA THE WAND. DON'T MISS US TOO MUCH!

Tonight Mal and I went back to Lady Tremaine's shop to find supplies for the smoke bombs. When we walked in, Dizzy tackle-hugged me. She was like my little sister on the Isle.

The Summer Solstice

When the sun's zenith
Is the farthest from the equator
And our North Pole tilts
Toward the mother star,
That day marks the solstice
In the Northern Hemisphere.

She had about a hundred questions about Auradon and what it was like there. Did I swim in a real swimming pool, and did they have walk-in closets? We caught up, and she showed me these spectacular hair accessories she's been designing. She uses materials she's scavenged off the streets, sometimes things she found in the trash— wire, broken watches, ripped fabric, metal scraps and beads. She puts it all together, sewing on lace strips and bows to make these beautiful creations. She even gave me a few to bring back to Auradon. I think people there will love them.

I told her I wish I could've brought her back to Auradon.
When I said it, she could barely look at me.

"At least one of us had our dream come true," she said.

When the sun stands still in our sky,
Witches and warlocks should celebrate,
Reveling in the <u>longest day of the year</u>.
Cleansing rituals are most effective
If performed in the last hour of this day,
And serums are most potent
If bottled and sealed
As the sun slips below the horizon.

IT FEELS like <u>THIS</u> IS THE lONGEST day OF THE YEAR. I CAN'T waiT UNTIL WE CAN GET BEN back. I hOPE hE'S okay.

Yeah, Dizzy will be okay on the Isle. She doesn't need me here.
But what about everything she's missing in Auradon?
<u>Doesn't she deserve the same opportunities I've had?</u>

YOU'RE RIGHT, EVIE, She dOES.

Dizzy even saved my old sketchbook, with all my designs from the Isle. I keep looking at it, thinking about how I could possibly help her. She's so incredibly talented, and so smart about all the different materials she uses and the different headpieces she's made. She's so much better than that dank dungeon of a place. There has to be something I can do. . . .

My Favorite Things about Dizzy's Designs

-She uses the coolest, most unique materials: watch gears, feathers, keys, lace, etc.

-They're all so HER. She has such a specific style and point of view.

-They can be dressed up or dressed down.

-They're well made. She puts such time and care into each one.

I hope not....

Dragon Bones

Crushed dragon bones
Are especially useful
In restoring strength and vitality.

The phalanges are best ground
With a mortar and pestle of white granite
And mixed with a python egg.

TONIGHT EVIE ASKED ME IF WHAT BEN AND I SHARED WAS TRUE LOVE. EVIE SAYS IT'S THE GREATEST MAGIC IN THE WORLD. THAT TRUE LOVE LASTS FOREVER.   It is!

THE TRUEST TRUTH IS ... I DON'T KNOW IF THAT'S WHAT WE HAVE. HOW CAN WE SEE INTO FOREVER? HOW CAN WE KNOW FOR SURE? WHEN I WAS WITH HIM, I FELT LIKE MY HEART WAS SO FULL. LIKE ANYTHING WAS POSSIBLE. AND NOW THAT HE'S IN DANGER ... I FEEL LIKE I'M IN DANGER, TOO. BUT IS THAT WHAT TRUE LOVE IS? OR IS IT SOMETHING MORE?

EVIE + DOUG

The caudal spade can be baked at 800 degrees
For ten hours, until it is ash,
Which can then be sprinkled over any dish.

Eat both before sunrise every morning
For seven days
After battle with an enemy.

True Love Is...

✓ Caring about someone deeply

Knowing everything about them and loving
them because of everything you know

✓ Feeling like they are your favorite person to be with
(besides your friends)

✓ Wanting the best for them no matter what

✓ Wishing your time with them could go on forever

✓ Feeling a special chemistry that exists with them
and only them (Love is its own sort of science.)

Mal—I thought about what you said, how you're not going back to Auradon with us, even if our plan works and we free Ben. Looking back, I can see how stressed out and unhappy you were. I'm just sorry that I wasn't a better friend, that I didn't realize how serious it was. If I knew you were really considering leaving Auradon for good . . .
I don't know, maybe we could've come up with a solution together.

YOU WERE A GOOD FRIEND, EVIE. YOU ALWAYS HAVE BEEN. AND I DON'T THINK ANYTHING YOU SAID WOULD'VE CHANGED MY MIND. THIS PRETTY PRINCESS IMAGE . . . THIS GIRL WHO IS ALWAYS ON CAMERA, WHO HAS TO BE A CERTAIN WAY . . . IT'S JUST NOT ME. IT NEVER WILL BE.

I TRIED TO RUN FROM THE TRUTH, BUT IT CAUGHT UP TO ME. THE ISLE OF THE LOST IS WHERE I BELONG. IT'S HOME.

We'll always be best friends, no matter what. We'll still talk—we have to. No matter how hard it is, no matter how far away you are, I'll always keep you in my heart.

And you'll always be in mine. That's a promise.

BEST FRIENDS FOREVER

Gross Goodies and Best Baddies

It is essential to know in whom you can confide
And who you must watch with a suspicious eye,
Waiting for their ultimate betrayal.

Peruse this list when determining your allies,
And commit these enemies to your everlasting memory.

A LOT HAS HAPPENED SINCE LAST NIGHT. JAY AND I TOOK THE LIMO BACK TO AURADON AND FOUND CHAD IN OUR ROOM, USING MY 3-D PRINTER. OF COURSE.

I WENT TO WORK PRINTING THE FAKE MAGIC WAND FROM A PICTURE ON MY PHONE. IF I'D NEVER SEEN THE REAL ONE UP CLOSE, I WOULD DEFINITELY THINK THIS IS THE REAL DEAL—THE ONLY THING THAT'S DIFFERENT IS THE WEIGHT. BUT THERE'S NO WAY FOR UMA TO KNOW THAT.

Best Baddies

The Evil Queen

Maleficent

Shan-yu

Jafar

Chernabog

Hades

Ursula the sea witch

Mother Gothel

Claude Frollo

Big Bad Wolf

Prince John

Scar

Cruella De Vil

Captain Hook

Amos Slade

Gaston

Stromboli

Kaa

Aunt Sarah

Madame Medusa

Lady Tremaine

Shere Khan

HER daughter is the WORST.

SO WE'D FINISHED UP AND WE WERE HEADING BACK TO THE LIMO WHEN LONNIE CAME UP TO US. SHE HAD THIS QUIVER FILLED WITH SWORDS. I THOUGHT SHE WAS GOING TO ASK JAY IF SHE COULD BE ON THE R.O.A.R. TEAM AGAIN, BUT SHE DEMANDED WE TAKE HER TO THE ISLE WITH US OR SHE WAS GOING TO TELL FAIRY GODMOTHER WHAT WE WERE DOING.... I GUESS FIVE IS BETTER THAN FOUR, RIGHT?!

Gross Goodies

Quasimodo

Prince Charming

Fairy Godmother

Pocahontas

Jasmine

Peter Pan

★ Mulan

Prince Eric

Aladdin

Perdita

Snow White

Rapunzel

Belle

Pongo

Hercules

Maid Marian

Beast

Cinderella

Li Shang

Robin Hood

Tiana

DEFINITELY.
MAL, EVIE—I KNOW YOU HAVEN'T SEEN LONNIE'S SWORD SKILLS YET, BUT WE'RE LUCKY TO HAVE HER WITH US. WHO KNOWS HOW MANY PIRATES WE'LL BE BATTLING?

PS: FORGOT TO MENTION . . . DUDE CAME ALONG, TOO. YOU'D THINK WITH HIS NEW VOCABULARY HE WOULD UNDERSTAND THE WORD "STAY." NOT. QUITE.

IT WAS SO BRAVE OF LONNIE TO COME WITH US. I MEAN, SERIOUSLY—SHE'S ONLY EVER SEEN THE ISLE OF THE LOST ON TV, AND IT'S NOT A PRETTY PICTURE. ALL SHE KNOWS IS THAT IT'S FILLED WITH VILLAINS WHO ARE READY TO TEAR EACH OTHER APART OVER A DIRTY LOOK. SHE DOESN'T KNOW THE STREETS, OR WHERE THE COVE IS, OR UMA'S STRENGTHS AND WEAKNESSES. SHE JUMPED INTO THIS TOTALLY BLIND, BECAUSE SHE KNEW WE COULD USE HER HELP.

I KEEP GOING BACK TO WHAT THE R.O.A.R. RULE BOOK SAID. "THE TEAM IS COMPOSED OF A CAPTAIN AND EIGHT MEN."

IS THERE ANY WAY AROUND THAT?

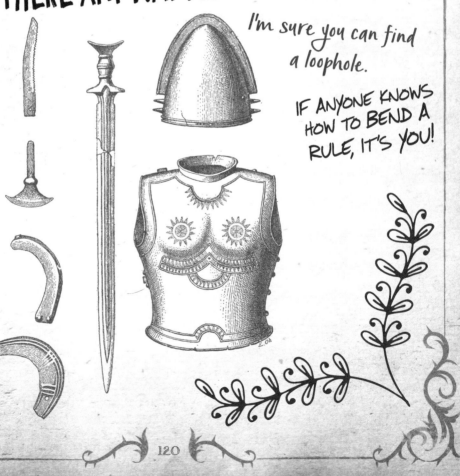

I'm sure you can find a loophole.

IF ANYONE KNOWS HOW TO BEND A RULE, IT'S YOU!

REASONS TO LET LONNIE ON THE R.O.A.R. TEAM:

-SHE'S A BETTER SWORDSPERSON THAN ANYONE I'VE EVER MET.

  -SHE'S A BETTER SWORDSPERSON THAN ME.

  -SHE'S BRAVE.

  -SHE'S A TEAM PLAYER.
    (SHE KNEW WE NEEDED HELP AND SHE VOLUNTEERED.)

-SHE TAKES INITIATIVE.

  -SHE'S CUNNING.

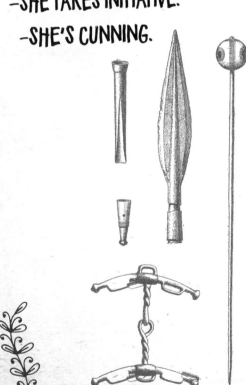

I remember one night, Doug took me firefly watching. He always manages to surprise me.

EVIE + DOUG FOREVER

TRUE LOVE = TRUE CHEMISTRY

Fireflies

Fireflies are a symbol of illumination
And the light within us all.
They appear on the banks of rivers
At sunset, their bodies blazing.

Strengthen your intuition
By standing among dozens
With closed eyes and open palms.
Then repeat these words:

Show me the way to myself.
Let the fire within be ignited.

Stones for Protection

These stones can protect
Even the most vulnerable souls
From misdeeds and devious intentions.

Carry them on your person
As close to the heart as possible.

I've lived on the Isle of the Lost almost my whole life. It takes a lot to shock me. But I can honestly say that when Lonnie stepped out of the limo with those swords on her back, I was completely and utterly surprised.

It's not that I didn't know Lonnie was amazing and fierce and brave and all those things. It's just that I always knew Evie, Carlos, and Jay would fight for me. And Ben was brave, sure, and more courageous than I ever thought he could be. But knowing that I made a friend in Auradon—a real friend, who would sacrifice so much to help—that's not something I'll ever take for granted.

Agate
Black kyanite
Black obsidian
Bloodstone
Celestite
Citrine
Elestial crystals
Emerald
Katanganite

Kunzite
Peacock ore
Peridot
Plancheite
Labradorite
Malachite
Schorl
Smoky quartz

I always carry an emerald on me for this reason. Evie even made a secret pocket in one of my jackets.

FUNNY THINGS DUDE HAS SAID

"DON'T TELL ME TO SIT. IT'S SO DEMEANING."

"WHAT IS THIS DISGUSTING MUCK YOU'VE BEEN FEEDING ME?"

"HAS CHAD ALWAYS BEEN THIS NEEDY?"

"IF I DON'T GET TO DIG A HOLE SOON, I'M GOING TO LOSE MY MIND."

"LET'S GO SNIFF SOME BUTTS."

"WOULD YOU WANT ME TO WALK YOU ON A LEASH?"

OH, IT'S TIME TO MEET UMA. GOTTA GO!

P.S. Dude just said blue is a very flattering color on me!

well, look what we have here. . . . so this is the little leather book Mal always carries with her. Her secret spell book, her and her friends' pathetic little diary. well, from here on out this is MY story—this is UMA's book now.

where to begin. . . . How about the moment my boys captured her pretty, preppy King Ben? Those VKs can dress him like a villain, but he was still a fish out of water on the Isle. It wasn't long before Harry snatched him up. How could they be so stupid to let Auradon's King out of their sight? He's the perfect bargaining chip for me.

I knew I'd beat Mal in the wrestling match, and I knew she'd have to bring me the magic wand. sure, she calls me shrimpy, like I'm some small, weak thing. But she's the one who's been drinking tea and planning silly parties, while I've been living the Isle life.

Fairy Tales for the Young

The Selfish Girl in the Red Cape

There once lived a cunning, brave wolf
who stalked the depths of the forest.
He was strong and fierce, but early one morning
he twisted his leg chasing a bunny.
The poor wolf spent days in his den, unable to hunt.
His foot ached.
His stomach growled.
He was so hungry his eyes watered from the pain.
Then, just when he thought he might starve,
he saw something strange.
In between the trees, there was a flash of red.

He could barely walk,
but he tried to follow the red cape.
It turned out to be a girl.
She was carrying a basket with biscuits,
pears, and a whole ham hock.
The wolf stared at the girl with pleading eyes,
but she just turned away from him.
She said she was going to her grandmother's house.
It was a cottage with a yellow front door.

The wolf knew the cottage with the yellow front door.
And he knew a shortcut through the woods
that would get him there first.
So he took off on the path, wincing with each step.
When he got to the cottage, a sweet old woman
opened the door, and he was so hungry
he gobbled her down whole.

After he was stuffed, he had to lie down and rest.
He put on a cozy nightgown and went to bed.
When he woke up, the girl with the red cape was there.
It didn't take long before he gobbled her down, too.

It wasn't his fault, was it?
He was so hungry he could barely think.
She should have just given him
some of those delicious biscuits when she had the chance.

This story always makes me so mad. They blamed _everything_ on the wolf without ever even hearing his side. That snobby Little Red Riding Hood had it coming, didn't she? Who was she to think she was better than the Big Bad Wolf?

The Strapping young Hero

This story takes place in a little town, a quiet village
where every day was like the one before.
In the village there lived a strong,
devastatingly handsome young man named Gaston.

Every girl in the entire village was
in love with Gaston.
Girls in neighboring villages were
in love with Gaston. *Gil's dad.*
But Gaston only had eyes for one
girl, and her name was Belle.

There was only one problem.
While all the other girls in the village
swooned when Gaston walked past,
Belle spent all her time reading,
riding her horse, or being with her father.
She acted like Gaston didn't even exist!

Every time Belle ignored Gaston, he was only
more certain that she was the girl for him.
Even when she turned down his marriage proposal,
he knew it was only a matter of time before
she changed her mind.
But then one day she was kidnapped by a horrible,
vicious beast who lived in a castle far from town.
Gaston took a bunch of his friends there and fought
the Beast until they were both tired and bloody.

Right before he struck his final blow, Gaston passed out.
He can't be completely sure what happened that night,
but he had to assume that he killed the evil beast.

That's not what happened.
Didn't anyone check this book for mistakes?!

As for Belle? No one ever heard from her again.
He thought about her for a while after he returned to
the village, but then there were so many other beautiful
girls who were in love with him . . .

It wasn't long before he married someone else.

Nothing felt better than beating Mal.
I always knew I was stronger and fiercer than her.
I've spent months watching clips of Mal on the Isle,
wondering what made her so special. Why did she get
to go to Auradon and not me? What does she have
that I don't?

The answer is: <u>NOTHING.</u> Nothing makes her special or better or more worthy. she just got lucky. And my plan was to get the magic wand and break down the barrier between the Isle and Auradon, letting all villain Kids rush in.

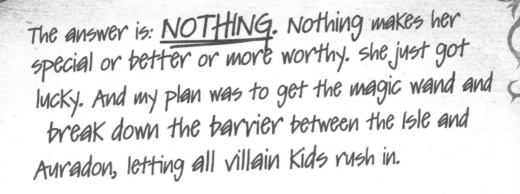

URSULA'S
FISH & CHIPS
You'll take it how I make it!

2 squid ink salads
1 basket of sea spiders
1 moray soufflé
2 cups pond scum

Total . . . 2 gold coins

(Paid with a gold tooth and a broken watch. Left a tip: copper mug.)

URSULA'S
FISH & CHIPS

You'll take it how I make it!

1 gruel smoothie
2 brine ball sandwiches

Total . . . 2 copper coins

(Paid for with a handful
of glass eyes. The
cheapskate didn't leave
a tip.)

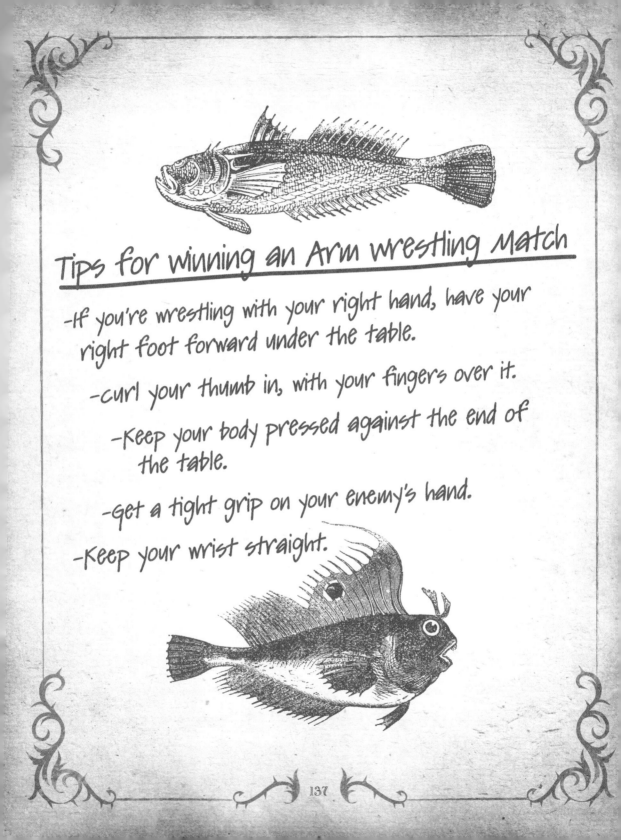

Tips for winning an Arm wrestling Match

-If you're wrestling with your right hand, have your right foot forward under the table.

-curl your thumb in, with your fingers over it.

-Keep your body pressed against the end of the table.

-get a tight grip on your enemy's hand.

-Keep your wrist straight.

Rules for Ursula's Fish & Chips Shoppe

-Employees must never wash their hands.

-Cockroaches are your friends.

-The customer is always wrong.

-Every dish tastes better with a little hair in it.

-Make them wait for a table, even if the place is empty.

-It should always smell of fish guts.

The Sea Witch

That's my mom!
At least Maleficent
recognized her power.

Far under the sea,
there once lived
a _cunning witch_, who took advantage
of poor unfortunate souls by the dozens.

One day, a young mermaid named Ariel
begged the powerful witch to help her become human.
So she gave Ariel legs
in exchange for Ariel's beautiful singing voice.
But of course, just being human wasn't enough
for the greedy little mermaid.
She wanted to be a princess, too,
so she tried to make a prince fall in love with her.

Ariel was so weak—
all that for some guy?

This gives me an idea. . . .

The sea witch couldn't have that.
So she transformed into a beautiful girl
and went on land and stole Ariel's prince.
They fell in love immediately,
for the sea witch was simply irresistible.

So, back to that sneaky _wannabe_ princess, Mal.
I'll admit it: even though I knew I'd beat her at the arm wrestling match and she'd have to get me the wand, I was a little shocked about Ben. He wasn't what I expected.

His father is the reason we're all here, trapped on the Isle. When King Beast came into power twenty years ago, he was the one who sent all the villains here to rot. There'd be no magic for us, no joy. Only bitterness and garbage piles (most of the time the sanitation department is on strike) and the feeling that you'll never be able to get out of this place, no matter how hard you try.

So I wasn't expecting anything from Ben, Beast's little spawn. I'd seen him speak on TV before, and in those clips he's always wearing his stuffy royal gear, and he's so formal. Stuck-up. But in real life he's got kind of a different vibe.

First, Mal and him are over. Done-zo. So I guess I can't hold that against him. Second, when I said how messed up it was that he only took four Isle kids over to Auradon, he actually listened, not interrupting or yelling like most Isle people would. He said his plan was to bring more Isle kids over, but then he got caught up with all his kingly responsibilities. He tried to give me an invite to Auradon. ("Thanks, but no thanks," I said. I have my own plans. . . .)

Maybe he's not as horrible as I thought. But he is still Beast's kid, and I still don't trust him.

The Two Sisters*

Two sisters named Anastasia and Drizella
lived in a big house with their mother, Lady Tremaine.
The three of them did everything together.
They dined in the fanciest restaurants, wore the fanciest
clothes, and went to parties with the fanciest people.

Then one day the sisters were invited to a royal ball.
The Prince was hoping to meet all the fairest maidens
and then make one of them his beautiful bride.
The sisters were dressed by their servant,
a pathetic girl named Cinderella.
(Maybe the girl was technically their stepsister,
but those are just small details.)

*That weak little Dizzy actually comes from a long line of wicked women. There's no excuse for her. With villain blood like that, she should be bossing people around, not sweeping floors in some wretched salon.

The servant had wanted to go to the ball, too,
but Lady Tremaine told her no.
Since when were lowly servants invited to royal balls?

That night, the sisters took a fancy coach to the
ball and greeted the Prince, curtsying in front of him.
It seemed like he might be charmed by one of them,
but then his eyes looked past them to a girl in a blue gown.
As soon as he saw her, he didn't stop looking at her all night.
He danced only with her.

When the two sisters finally went home,
they were heartbroken.
The Prince had barely even looked at them.
The sisters tried not to think of it too much.
But then one day the king's men came to the door,
this time with a glass slipper.
The girl in the blue gown had left it behind
without telling anyone her name.

Keeping villains in Line

- Always make sure your minions fear you.
- Always make them shout your name.
- Always make them do the dirty work
- Never explain yourself.
- Never reveal your entire plan to them.
- Never let them talk about you behind your back

It didn't fit the two sisters, but it did fit Cinderella,
who insisted on trying it on.
She was immediately whisked away to the castle
to be married to the Prince.
They still live there, happily ever after.

If only Cinderella had tripped and broken her neck
as she ran down the stairs.

Things I'd Actually Eat at Mom's Shop

1. Seaweed soda

2. Dogfish dumplings

3. Sea horse soup

4. Basket of fried smelts

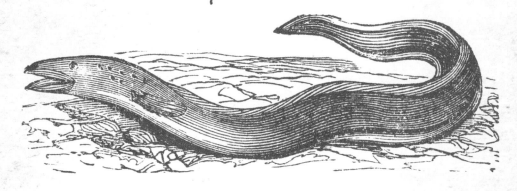

5. crab crunch (It's a sandwich special where you eat the whole crab: shell and all.)

Anatomy of a Pirate Ship

Spanker sail

Main topsail

Poop deck

Mainsail

Fore topsail

Foresail

Foredeck

Stern

Anchor

Bow

Bowsprit

Main Deck

Rudder

Things were going my way until Mal and her gang showed up with that wand. The clock struck noon.

When Mal came over the bridge, I saw the wand in her hand. It looked exactly like the one I'd seen a hundred times on TV, the one that uppity Fairy Godmother was always waving around. Even though I recognized the turquoise jewel in the bottom of it and all the fancy-schmancy gold stuff, I made her do a little demonstration. (My pirate minions love watching me tell people what to do.)

And when she pointed the wand at that little rat dog Carlos carries around, the dog started talking. I'm still not sure how she got the little fleabag to do that. . . . Do all dogs in Auradon talk?

Poor Unfortunate Souls:
How to Prey on the Weak

Befriending a tortured soul may be beneficial
If they have something to offer you for your alliance
Follow these rules for the most devious plotting.

After that I was convinced the wand was the real deal.
Ripped out of Fairy Godmother's manicured hands.

I'd prepared spells just for that moment. I held up the wand, pointing at the barrier, and recited one . . . Nothing. Absolutely nothing. The spell hadn't even caused a ripple in the barrier—it looked exactly the same.

So I tried the next one.

-DO be patient.
-DO pretend you are their ally.
-DO promise help to the person in need.
-DO observe their weaknesses.
-DO consider what they have to offer you.
-DON'T ever reveal your true intentions.
-DON'T ever reveal your weaknesses.
-DON'T ask directly for what you want.

Still nothing. That's when I realized what had happened: those sneaky little twerps had given me a fake wand.

AGGGHHHHHHHH!!!!

I hate her!!

After that, chaos broke out. Mal's friends threw a bunch of smoke bombs, which exploded in front of us in clouds of bright colors. It was impossible to keep track of all of them.

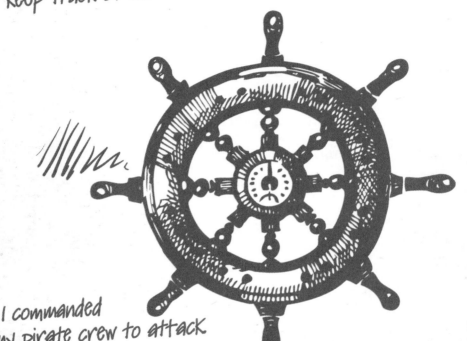

I commanded my pirate crew to attack. They are fierce and didn't hesitate for even a second. Harry and I quickly followed. I met nasty old Mal on the docks, and we had a face-off. Somehow, she and her little friends were suddenly armed to the teeth in swords. But I'm a pirate. And I know how to use a sword. It was almost cute how she blocked my blows. Around us on the docks, my band of pirates hacked away at Mal's little group.

I decided to end it then and there. But Mal stepped on my sword and took off up the docks.

I found Harry, and the two of us charged after her. I went in, swinging at Mal again with my sword while Harry homed in on Ben. Just when I thought I had Mal beat, her prissy princess friend Evie chucked a smoke bomb and everything went dark

When the smoke cleared, Mal's friends had vanished into the pipe tunnel. Mal stood at its entrance, smirking. She kicked out the bridge that connected the tunnel to the docks. Nothing has ever made me madder. And that's saying a lot! She vanished into the tunnel and I stormed back to my ship. I may have lost the battle, but the war is far from over.

WATCH OUT, MAL. IT'S NOT OVER YET.

TRAITOR

MALEFICENT'S DAUGHTER TO BE NAMED LADY OF THE COURT

Infatuation Spell

He doesn't notice your beautiful eyes
Or whisper sweet nothings
About the stars in the sky.
He doesn't give you his hand when you walk
Or lean in close, enthralled when you talk.
Will he ever kiss your sweet little cheek?
Will he ever give all the affection you seek?

If your patience has grown thin,
This infatuation spell will reel him in.

This is JUST what I need.

Thanks, Mal.

Yes, Ben and Mal may have taken off, proving what wimpy cowards they are.

They thought they were so smart, tricking me. But I'm gonna have the last evil laugh.

Because now I'm in Auradon, where all the magic happens. Literally. Apparently, Mal is going to be named lady of the court at something called the cotillion. Or at least that was what was supposed to happen.

I say, not so fast, Mal. There's only room for one of us. . . .

On a piece of decade=old parchment
Write down the name of the beloved.
Sprinkle with sand from a beach at low tide
And submerge in water, reciting these words:

Make his love as deep as the ocean.
May he see all the wonder I possess
And celebrate it in every minute
With every sunrise and sunset.

I am so looking forward to getting back at Mal for all the things she's done to me. For all the times she laughed at me and called me Shrimpy. For all the days and weeks I ran around my mother's shop, serving chips to rude customers while Mal was here in Auradon, going to fancy banquets and dances and learning how to be a lady. For all the times I saw her on TV, smiling into those cameras like she was so much better than the people she left behind.

When I saw the way Mal and Ben looked at each other, how he jumped in front of her, trying to protect her, I knew . . . I'd take away her one true love. What better way to get revenge than to crash the Auradon Cotillion and steal Mal's boyfriend? What better way to show Auradon, and the entire world, that I won?!

JUST WHAT I THOUGHT.
IT ALL MAKES SENSE NOW....

I can't believe she was plotting away in OUR spell book OUR Villain-Kid-None-of-Your-Business book. It's ruined!

SHE COULD NEVER RUIN WHAT WE HAVE.
WE'RE STRONGER THAN THAT. FOUR HEARTS!

Piracy 101

- A pirate dresses like a pirate. Boots, scarves, pirate hats, and leather jackets. Eye patches, hooks, daggers, and swords.

- A pirate lives on a pirate ship.

  - A pirate says things like "you're a scallywag, you ol' sea dog," "walk the plank," and "Ahoy, matey!"

- A pirate travels to foreign lands to seize what they want.

~~UMA~~
~~LADY MAL~~
to Make her
OFFICIAL DEBUT
at the Auradon
Cotillion

EXCLUSIVE
PHOTO

I wish I had time to make this before the Cotillion. . . .

Elixir of Strength

In a bronze cauldron
Combine a <u>minced lion's heart</u>
With one cup water
From a well on a line of power.
Mix in two teaspoons
Of dust from a witch's broom
And let sit for three days.

where would I even find this in Auradon?

Consume this elixir
On the third day at midnight
To summon the strength
Of ten angry warlocks.

Mal, a.k.a. . . .

Princess Prim and Proper

Lady of the Phonies

Princess Smug Face

Shark Snack

Lizard Kin

Traitor

Turns out I can come up with some pretty good nicknames, too, huh?

Fairy Godmother Spell

"Bibbidi-Bobbidi-Boo," she said
With a wave of her magic wand.

You might not have the tools she did
But you can still manage to transform.

In a large bronze bowl
Combine three teaspoons of crushed honeysuckle,
A cup of ground pumpkin seeds,
And two tears of human joy.
Mix well and smear over a mirror
Framed in gold and silver

GUYS. I'M CRUSHING ON THE DAUGHTER OF A FAIRY.
I NEVER WOULD HAVE IMAGINED THAT, NOT EVEN IN MY
WILDEST DREAMS, WHEN I WAS LIVING ON THE ISLE.

As you incant:

YEAH, OUR LIVES ARE
PRETTY CRAZY NOW.
BUT I KIND OF DIG IT!

Bring me beauty, head to toe,
A look that is sure to impress.
Bring me grace, head to toe,
And a big poufy evening dress.

Harry and Gil should be in this book, too—
after all, they're part of my crew. Here are
some of my favorite memories of them:

That time we threw an after-hours dance party
at Mom's shop.

That time Gil laughed so hard he squirted a seaweed shake
out of his nose.

That time we went swimming in the harbor at night.

That time we found an old lady's purse.
(Okay, she was wearing it.)

That time Harry got me a stolen radio for my birthday.

That time Gil gave me a
piggyback ride to the pawn
shop.

Oh— gotta go. They're calling me for my
big Auradon cotillion entrance.
I'd say "Wish me luck," but I don't need it. . . .

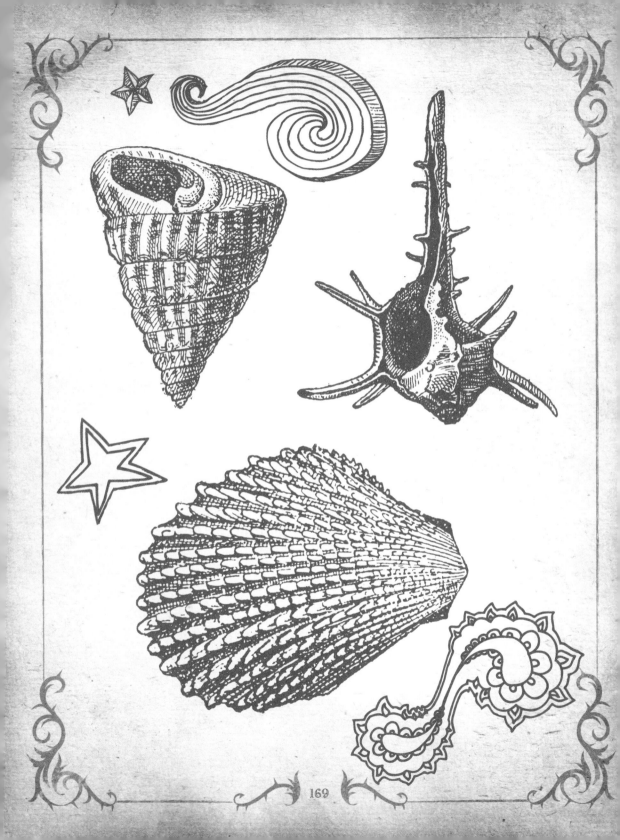

I wish I could make some of this to help restore my strength. I swore off using spells, though....

Hawk Feather Elixir

The feathers of the red female hawk
Are invaluable in regaining strength
After battle with a fierce enemy.

They're most effective
When boiled in water from a giant's well.

Strain the elixir and mix in 2 pinches of ocean salt
And a single cat hair.
Drink the concoction down in three gulps.
Rest two sunsets and feel your full power.

IT'S GOOD TO HAVE MY SPELL BOOK BACK.

IT FEELS LIKE OUR WHOLE HISTORY IN AURADON IS IN THESE PAGES. ALL OF MY FRIENDS' THOUGHTS AND MEMORIES. EVERYTHING THAT HAS HAPPENED TO US (AND APPARENTLY SOME THINGS THAT HAPPENED TO UMA?!).

I'M GRATEFUL THAT FG LET US WRITE A LITTLE MORE IN THIS BOOK BEFORE SHE PUTS IT IN THE MUSEUM. SO MUCH HAS HAPPENED SINCE WE LEFT THE ISLE. I ALMOST DON'T KNOW WHERE TO BEGIN FINISHING THIS STORY!!

I do! How about we start with our big talk the day of the cotillion? How we all shared our feelings?

FEELINGS. GROSS.

SPEAK FOR YOURSELF! I THOUGHT I WAS PRETTY GOOD AT "GIRL TALK."

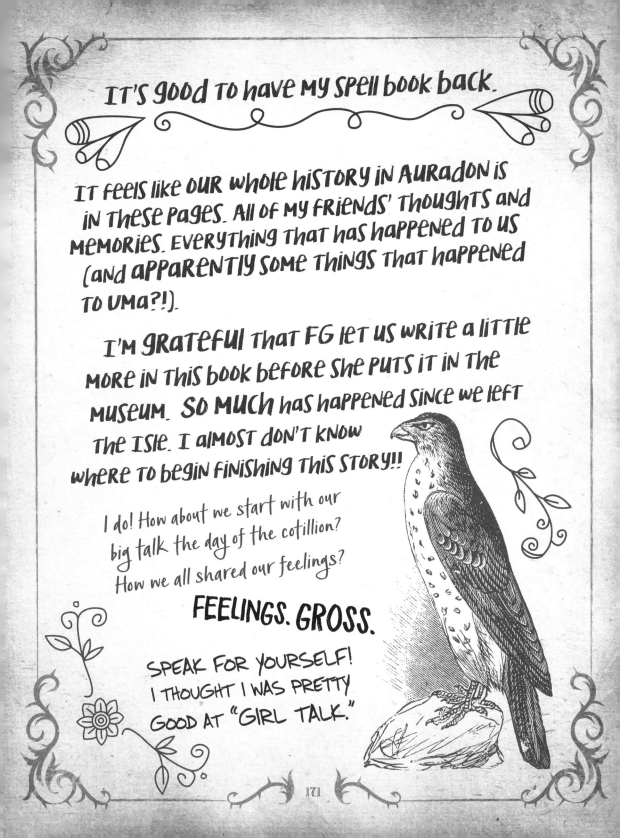

Beware <u>True</u> <u>Love's</u> Kiss

A kiss from one's true love
Is the enemy of any dark spell.

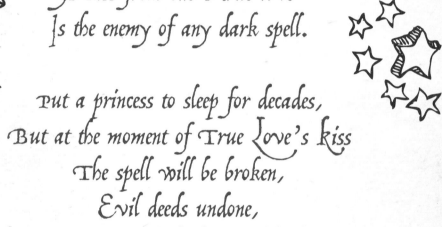

Put a princess to sleep for decades,
But at the moment of True Love's kiss
The spell will be broken,
Evil deeds undone,
The most cunning witch thwarted in her quest.

Told you it was powerful, Mal!

YOU WERE RIGHT.

So once we got back to Auradon, we all sat down and had a serious talk. (Oh, and Dude, too. He had some stuff to say.) Mal said all the things she'd been thinking and feeling. Listening to her talk, I really understood. Because the truth is we ARE different. We are never going to fit in perfectly here in Auradon, because we're not from Auradon. We're from the Isle. Nothing we can do will undo all we've seen and experienced.

We all decided to be ourselves, no matter what. To try to stay true to where we are from. Not by being bad, but by being okay with being a little different. And for Mal, that means showing Ben the REAL her. Without that silly lady's manners book and this spell book and the blonde hair and everything. For me? It means bringing some more Isle to Auradon. I wasted no time with my designs, changing up Mal's dress and adding Dizzy's hair accessories to some of the gown I'd made. Because nothing says Isle style like a hair accessory made out of screws and broken watch parts. Seriously... they're crazy beautiful.

HE ALWAYS HAS STUFF TO SAY. LITTLE MAN WILL NOT SHUT UP.

JUST THIS MORNING HE WAS LIKE: "I THINK YOU'D LOOK MUCH BETTER WITH PINK HAIR." ????

Reunion Spell

The witch and her lost dragon . . .
An evil queen and a lovesick king . . .
Loves who are miles apart . . .

To bring them together
Recite this whenever
The moon is full and bright:

THE BIG NEWS SINCE I LAST WROTE IN HERE IS THAT . . .
DRUMROLL, PLEASE . . . I FINALLY ASKED JANE TO THE
COTILLION. IT STILL TOOK ME ABOUT THREE TRIES TO GET IT
RIGHT (OR FOR HER TO UNDERSTAND JUST WHAT I WAS ASKING).
BUT IT HAPPENED. AND SHE SAID YES.

WE WERE REALLY PROUD OF YOU CARLOS!

THAT'S WHAT BEING ME IN AURADON MEANS. BEING BRAVE.
TAKING CHANCES. AND NOT BEING AFRAID TO SAY WHO
I AM AND WHAT I WANT TO BE OR DO.

PS: I FORGOT TO MENTION . . . DUDE GAVE ME THIS REALLY FUNNY PEP TALK. HE TOLD ME ALL ABOUT THIS POODLE HE USED TO BE IN LOVE WITH, AND HOW HE NEVER TOOK THE RISK AND SHOWED HER. HE SAID IF ONLY HE COULD'VE TALKED THEN, HE WOULD'VE RECITED THE MOST ROMANTIC POETRY TO HER. HAHA

Before the dawn
You will be drawn
Into each other's sight.

Before the dawn
You will be drawn
Into each other's sight.

AFTER we all talked, EVERYTHING SEEMED SO MUCH CLEARER. I knew I had to show BEN THE REAL ME, and I had to show all of AURADON, TOO. I COULDN'T KEEP UP MY blonde hair and THESE PRIM MANNERS and THIS IMAGE of THE PERFECT lady. If AURADON WANTED ME TO be THE lady of THE COURT, I had TO show up as MYSELF.

SO EVIE MADE MY DRESS as "Mal" as POSSIBLE. AND I walked INTO THE COTILLION WITH bRIGHT PURPLE hair and leATHER bRACELETS ON MY WRISTS. I held MY head up high, even though I was SO NERVOUS about what THEY WOULD THINK . . . and what BEN WOULD THINK.

TURNS OUT BEN didN'T NOTICE. NOT REALLY. BECAUSE UMA was his date TO THE COTILLION. He came down THE STAIRS, UMA JUST a MINUTE behind him, and he announced her TO EVERYONE. She was even wearing his RING. I had TO take a deep breATH so I didN'T CRY. AFTER SPENDING SO MANY hours getting ready, imagining dancing with BEN and holding his hand and TELLING him JUST how I felt . . .

IT was JUST TOO MUCH.

I've never been so angry in my entire life. I just kept staring at him, like: WHAT ARE YOU THINKING?! HOW COULD YOU DO THIS?! AND HOW DID SHRIMPY GET INTO AURADON?!

I WAS REALLY NOT HAPPY WE RISKED OUR LIVES FOR HIM. NOT. AT. ALL.

HE'S LUCKY I DIDN'T HAVE MY SWORD.

~~Beauty Potion~~

Beauty comes from within. It's about being true to yourself and knowing who you are.

Yellow teeth,

Frizzy hair,

A complexion that's oily and pink...

Turn puffy pimples

Into cute little dimples

While fixing your breath (which stinks!)

In a silver chalice

Mix the following ingredients:

THAT WASN'T EVEN THE WORST PART. Jane had spent weeks helping Ben make a special surprise for me to be unveiled at the cotillion. She was so confused when Uma showed up, but she announced the surprise anyway. The curtain fell, revealing a stained glass window of me and Ben.

Together. Happy. Frozen in time as we kissed.

The best part was it was the real me, with purple hair and Isle style and all the things I thought Ben didn't like. He had always known me and he loved me. He really loved me.

So I was horrified when Ben commanded Fairy Godmother to bring down the barrier.

Then I realized... Uma had spelled Ben. I rushed forward to tell him how I truly felt, knowing there was only one thing that could break

2 hairs from a unicorn's tail

½ teaspoon powdered dragon bone

The minced liver of an owl

1 cup of water from an enchanted lake

Swallow one sip every night for five nights

Starting on the night of the full moon.

Monitor your transformation in a magic mirror

And repeat as often as necessary.

Uma's spell. I explained why I hadn't told him I loved him when he came to the hideout, how I had been scared.

And then I kissed him—TRUE LOVE'S KISS.

It totally worked. Within seconds, Ben came back to himself.

He came back to ME.

I couldn't believe what happened next. Uma swiped at Fairy Godmother's wand. Fairy Godmother called for the guards to seize her. But Uma ran to the side of the yacht and jumped into the water below. Using the magic from her mother's shell necklace, Uma rose from the water—transformed into a giant sea monster! She had long tentacle arms like Ursula, and she towered over the yacht, making it look so small beside her. Then she swiped the boat deck and nearly threw me overboard. I jumped back just in time.

I thought that was it, that she'd destroy us all. I turned to Mal because I was so scared. But she looked completely different. Her eyes glowed a deep green. Mal rose up in a cloud of smoke and transformed into the fiercest dragon I've ever seen.

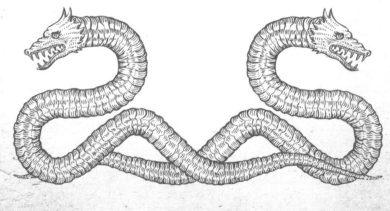

IT WAS INCREDIBLE. MAL CHARGED TOWARD UMA, READY FOR BATTLE. RIGHT BEFORE THEY WERE ABOUT TO FIGHT, BEN DOVE INTO THE WATER BETWEEN THEM AND CALLED FOR PEACE. HE YELLED, "FIGHTING WON'T BRING THE ISLE AND AURADON TOGETHER!" THEN HE TOLD EVERYONE TO LISTEN TO AND RESPECT EACH OTHER. GOTTA SAY, IT WAS A PRETTY BOLD MOVE ON MY MAN BEN'S PART.

UMA GOT THIS STRANGE, SAD LOOK ON HER FACE BEFORE SHE DOVE BACK INTO THE WATER. I ALMOST FELT A LITTLE BAD FOR HER — ALMOST.

SHE SWAM TOWARD THE ISLE AND DISAPPEARED.

ADMIT ONE

AURADON COTILLION
Saturday at Eight O'Clock
in the Evening

True Love Yacht

AURADON
A P
PREP

The Wrath of Dragons

THIS IS SO TRUE! YOU WERE INCREDIBLE, MAL. EVEN I WAS SCARED OF YOU.

There is nothing fiercer
Than a snarling dragon,
That winged lizard,
Nostrils flared,
Fiery breath.

WATCHING MAL TURN INTO A DRAGON— I THINK THAT MIGHT'VE BEEN THE COOLEST THING I'LL EVER SEE IN MY LIFE.

Dragons have been known
To possess strength a thousand times
That of the average witch or warlock,
Making transformation a vital skill.

EVIE'S 4 HEARTS SHINES ON COTTILIION RED CARPET

The designer accessorized with headpieces from Dizzy of the Isle.

GREAT JOB WITH THOSE OUTFITS, EVIE. I'VE NEVER SEEN AURADON PREP STUDENTS LOOK SO SHARP.

EVERYBODY WAS RELIEVED WHEN UMA DISAPPEARED. FROM THAT MOMENT ON, THE COTILLION WAS A huge SUCCESS. THERE WAS MUSIC AND DANCING, AND I EVEN loved THE CENTERPIECES AND PEN TOPPERS. (APPARENTLY, I MADE SOME good CHOICES THERE. I'M NOT so bad AS LADY OF THE COURT.)

AND DESPITE MY DRAGON TRANSFORMATION, EVIE'S DESIGNS WERE THE REAL STAR OF THE NIGHT. PEOPLE ARE STILL RAVING ABOUT THE DRESSES SHE MADE, AND HOW COOL DIZZY'S HAIR ACCESSORIES WERE. LAST NIGHT, ON THE BOAT DECK, DANCING WITH BEN, I FELT HAPPY IN AURADON AGAIN . . . like ANYTHING WAS POSSIBLE. Anything IS possible here. We're glad you're back, Mal.

Incense

Incense can have beneficial properties.
The smoldering embers
Fill the room with delightful scents.
Use the following incenses for these purposes:

Cedarwood: Brings strength, power
Anise: Emotional balance
Ginger: Encourages desire
Cardamom: Confidence, courage
Lavender: Beauty

IT WAS A CRAZY NIGHT, IN THE BEST WAY.
I KNOW I'VE NEVER BEEN TO A MORE FUN PARTY.

I SHOULD MENTION HERE, FOR THE OFFICIAL RECORD:
LONNIE IS NOW THE CAPTAIN OF THE R.O.A.R. TEAM.
AFTER WE CAME BACK FROM THE ISLE, I COULDN'T
STOP THINKING ABOUT HOW BRAVE AND
FIERCE SHE WAS.

Ben was right.
The people of the Isle and Auradon will
always be enemies if we keep fighting.

~~Ylang-Ylang~~: Harmony and euphoria

Cinnamon: Raising energy

Nutmeg: Attracting prosperity

Gardenia: Healing

Violet: Fosters wisdom, luck

Frankincense: Brings calm, peace

Sandalwood: Purifying properties

Pine: Grounding properties

Vanilla: Intelligence, clarity of thought

WHO WOULD BE A BETTER TEAMMATE THAN LONNIE?
WHO HAD THE CRAZY SWORDSPERSON SKILLS SHE HAD?

NO ONE.

SO I DID THE AURADON THING—I DIDN'T BREAK THE
RULES. I JUST, ERRRR ... REINTERPRETED THEM.
IF THE TEAM IS COMPOSED OF A CAPTAIN AND EIGHT
MEN, COULDN'T LONNIE BE OUR CAPTAIN?

Doug and I had a great night, for sure. After all the running around, getting orders ready for Evie's 4 Hearts, it was clear that all our hard work had been worth it. All the dresses looked incredible on the red carpet. The best part is now everyone sees how talented Dizzy is, not just me. I keep imagining her in Lady Tremaine's shop, seeing all her hair accessories on TV. I wish I could've been there to give her a hug.

I told Ben all about her, and about the other kids on the Isle who deserve a chance at a new life. I wasn't sure what he'd say, but he agreed to let me lead the committee that decides who to bring over. I'm supposed to be putting together a list.

I already know who will be at the top of it....

They even looked GREAT soaking wet. BRAVO, EVIE!

186

COULD IT BE? IS IT TRUE LOVE?

MY DATE WITH JANE WAS ONE OF THE BEST NIGHTS I'VE HAD SINCE I CAME TO AURADON. NO, THAT'S NOT RIGHT—IT <u>WAS</u> THE BEST. THINGS WERE MORE MAGICAL THAN THAT MAGIC WAND.

I DID NOT like that one bit. →

He was spelled, Evie. We can't blame him. . . .

IT DIDN'T MATTER THAT UMA SHOWED UP, OR THAT BEN ALMOST BROKE MAL'S HEART, OR THAT A GIANT WAVE CRASHED DOWN ON THE DECK AFTER UMA TURNED INTO A SEA WITCH. IT ONLY TOOK ONE DANCE TO MAKE ALL OF THAT FEEL VERY FAR AWAY. I DON'T KNOW WHAT WILL HAPPEN WITH US, OR WHAT'S GOING TO HAPPEN TOMORROW. BUT THESE LAST FEW DAYS IN AURADON, WELL, DUDE WASN'T THE ONLY ONE WHO FOUND HIS VOICE.

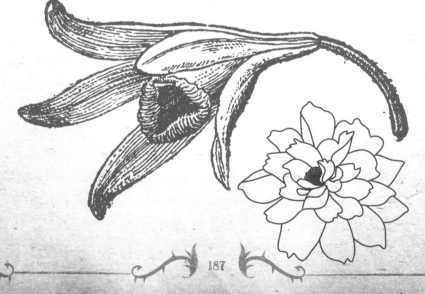

SO MUCH HAS CHANGED IN JUST THE LAST DAY. IT SEEMS like EVERYTHING I THOUGHT ABOUT BEN AND ME WAS WRONG. HE DOESN'T WANT ME TO BE SOME BORING PRISS WHO ALWAYS DOES THE RIGHT THING. HE JUST WANTS ME TO BE ME—WHICH IS GOOD, BECAUSE THAT'S ALL I'VE WANTED, TOO.

Herbs

Herbs have medicinal properties
And can be used to heal the infirm.
Collect the following herbs in copious amou
To store for treatment of these ailments:

Elder: Treats cold symptoms
Peppermint: Indigestion
Garlic: Antibacterial properties
Echinacea: Immunity booster

??? ??

Designs by Dizzy

That's why we're RETIRING this spell book, once and for all. It'll have a nice home in the MUSEUM OF CULTURAL HISTORY, right next to my MOM'S SPINDLE and EVIE'S MAGIC MIRROR. I've loved writing in this book with you guys, but I'll love it MORE if I don't have to think about it anymore or WORRY about what spell I need to make me do whatever it is I think I need to do. Those days are over.

Good. Farewell, spell book, we'll miss you!

Calendula: Heals wounds

IT'S BEEN REAL, SPELL BOOK.

Valerian: Sleeping disorders

Ginger: Treats motion sickness

Mullein: Treats sore throat

Hawthorn: Promotes heart health

Chamomile: Encourages digestion

Marshmallow: Treats sore throat

Comfrey: Treats bruises, sprains

Yarrow: Reduces inflammation

YOU'LL ALWAYS HOLD A SPECIAL PLACE IN MY HEART.

MINE TOO.

To the visitors of the Museum of Cultural History—

This is a very special spell book. It once belonged to Maleficent, a powerful fairy who was cast out of this kingdom. The book was inherited by her daughter, Mal, who was ultimately brought to Auradon on King Ben's orders. He founded an initiative to give villain kids more opportunities in this land.

Mal and her friends Evie (the Evil Queen's daughter), Carlos (Cruella De Vil's son), and Jay (Jafar's son) used this book as a journal to write back and forth to one another. We hope you find it invaluable in understanding their part in Auradon's rich history.